J. Dyer Ball

Macao

Salzwasser

J. Dyer Ball

Macao

1. Auflage | ISBN: 978-3-84604-870-2

Erscheinungsort: Frankfurt, Deutschland

Erscheinungsjahr: 2020

Salzwasser Verlag GmbH

Reprint of the original, first published in 1905.

MACAO:

The Holy City;

The Gem of the Orient Earth;

By

J. Dyer Ball, M. R. A. S.

Author of
Things Chinese,
The Cantonese Made Easy Series,
How to Write Chinese,
Hakka Made Easy,
&c., &c., &c.,

———◦———

Printed by
The China Baptist Publication Society
Canton.

1905

CONTENTS

MACAO

Geographical Position

The Portuguese Colony of Macao is situated on a rocky peninsula in the Heung Shan (Fragrant Hills) District in the Kwong Chau Prefecture of the Kwong Tung, or Canton Province, in the south eastern part of the Empire of China. This peninsula forms the most southerly point of the large Island of Heung Shan, this latter being one of the countless islands lying in the estuary of the Canton River on its western side. Macao is situated in 22 degrees, 11 minutes, 30 seconds, N. lat. and 113 degrees 32 minutes, 30 seconds, E. long. It and Hongkong, from which it is distant 40½ miles in a westerly direction, may be considered as the extreme points of the base of an obtuse angled triangle of which Canton, distant some 88 miles in a northerly direction, forms the apex, the line drawn from Hongkong, about 90 miles in length, being the hypothenuse. The whole peninsula on which Macao is built is about 3 miles long from the extreme point which the steamers round on passing from the outer to the inner harbour to the long narrow isthmus of sand where Macao is joined to the Chinese empire and less than a mile in breadth and the circuit is said to be about 8 miles. On this peninsula are two principal ranges of hills running north and south and east and west respectively. They rise from 200 to 300 feet in height. Besides all the hilly portions which lend such a variety to the *coup d'œul* and throw up into prominence the public and private edifices crowning their heights or built on their sides, are numerous tracts of level land largely utilised for the erection of houses. Not only does the hilly nature of the peninsula give more variety to the scene; but the chance of a breeze is also enhanced by the rising ground on which the rows of houses climb and detached residencies are perched. Several forts crown the different heights and churches as well as other public buildings are by no means wanting.

Many a picturesque view is to be obtained, the fine sweep of the the Praya Grande being universally admired.

The streets are kept bautifully clean and the public and private buildings are often gaily coloured.

All lovers of poetry and literature will cherish Macao as being at one time, the residence of the celebrated Portuguese poet Camoens. The climate is pleasant and there is but little bustle and noise; so being within convenient reach of Hongkong and Canton it forms a pleasent retreat for those who are seeking rest and quiet.

Census

The population of Macao is composed principally of Chinese which section is an ever increasing one owing to house-rent being cheaper than in Hongkong and life and property being more secure under the rule of the Portuguese officials than under the regime of the generally rapacious Chinese Mandarin in Canton and its neighbourhood. This Chinese portion of the population had increased in the 18 years between 1878 and 1897 by 11,036. A comparison of different censuses and estimates of population may prove of interest as showing how the once small Portuguese settlement has grown to a large populous city and colony.

A. D. 1583 Macao contained 900 Portuguese, "besides women, slaves and many hundreds of Chinese children" "and a great many people who came from Portuguese ports in Asia."

Latter end of the 17th Century the population of Macao amounted to 19,500.

A. D. 1821, 4557 or 4600.

A. D. 1830, about 4628.

A. D. 1824, 5093.

A. D. 1874, Portuguese, 4476; Foreigners, 78; Chinese, 63,532; Total, 68,086.

A. D. 1897, Portuguese, 3898; Foreigners, 161; Chinese, 74,627, Total, 78,706.

That the number of the Chinese in Macao was not larger at first is to be partly accounted for by the policy pursued by the Portuguese in the earlier days of the Settlement as it was considered wiser to limit their numbers. By thus keeping down the numbers in 1697 to only those registered and ordering all others to leave the city in three days, the refractory being handed over to the mandarins as vagabonds, it was doubtless hoped to keep Macao from being the happy hunting ground of the Canton lower classes, from the lawlessness of whom, brought down by hundreds, through the facilities of early transit, Hongkong in later days has often suffered. This policy however, actuated by the best of motives, proved unavailing, the landlords though forbidden by law (A. D. 1749) to let or sell their houses to Chinese, still doing so; in consequence of which this order of the senate was overruled in 1793.

City Walls

In the olden days when Macao was growing into a place of greater importance it was felt necessary to protect it from the assaults of covetous enemies and it was determined that a wall should be erected for that purpose.

One writer informs us that the open consent of the Chinese officials was first sought by a deputation from Macao but failing this, largesses prevented the corrupt mandarins from awkward objections or a hostile attitude to the undertaking: so that in A. D. 1622 a wall was run from the Monte (the height in the centre of the penuisula) in a north easterly direction to the sea near St. Francis and, it is stated, the work might have been completed in A. D. 1626. This wall may still be seen. It starts from the Place of Luiz Camoens. At this point the author remembers a small arched gate, the San Antonio gate, (Sam Pa Mun) which was closed at night. This has now

been pulled down and the road widened. From this place
the wall runs along and then up the hill to the Monte Fort
from whence it runs down the hill on the opposite side
where at the foot there used to be another gate, that of San
Francisco, now also abolished. The wall from here runs
up the opposite hill towards the sea, to the ruined fort of
San Joao, whence it proceeds towards San Francisco fort.
which lies at one end of the Praya Grande, then running
along the side of the Estrada da San Francisco down the
hill facing the fort, mentioned above, where it ends. Thus
the city was entirely closed on the land side. Some Dutch
prisoners taken in 1622 were employed in the building of
this wall.

Another short city wall is to be seen to the south of the
city. It runs from the church on Penha Hill to the road
above the disused Bom Parto Fort or just about opposite
the old Boa Vista Hotel.

The Barrier

This is the division between Portuguese and Chinese
territory. It is some distance along the long isthmus
which unites the peninsula of Macao to China.

To reach it from the Macao Hotel you pass the Public
Gardens at the end of the Praya Grande on your right hand
and keep straight on, passing a number of Chinese houses;
before quite reaching the end of these houses you turn to
the right and then to the left along a boulevard, on your
left being the open Campo or a Chinese village, &c. The
boulevard ended you pass in front of barracks and then the
Governor of Macao's country house set in a garden. You
keep on in the same direction, bearing a bit to the left until.
the road comes out on the sea. Turn to the left and follow
the road till a road, leading directly to the Barrier Gate.
down the centre of the isthmus, turns to the right.

Soon after passing the Governor's summer residence a
road turns to the right which leads to Cacilha's Bay with a
pretty little sandy beach. Above the road and the Bay is the
Plague Burying Ground, the graves marked by wooden

crosses. By this road one may return to the Praya Grande at a distance of several hundred feet above the sea.

But to return to the road which leads to the Barrier. Just before coming in sight of the sea one sees to the left enclosed in a wall, the new Protestant Burying Ground. The old Protestant Cemetery is below the Protestant Chapel, next Camoen's gardens.

Below the new cemetery are the courts of the Macao tennis club.

Just before reaching the Barrier a short distance is the bathing place, the whole coast line here forming with the sandy beach on the seaward side a magnificent roughly semi-circular bay. Many large fishing stakes are seen with the hovels of their owners perched up amongst the rocks. The whole of Macao seems dominated by forts. To the left is a large one, topping a hill, commanding the Barrier, while to the left are two small ones overlooking the sea and Cacilha's Bay. Once on the road, leading to the Barrier, we see facing us the large gateway which marks the boundary line. As already said the sandy beach is below us on the right with some rough grassy ground between. The muddy shores of the Inner Harbour on the left and on the falling or lower ground between the road and the water, the ever-industrious Chinese market-gardener has brought his skill to bear and the result is beautiful plots of vegetables, planted in symmetrical rows, lovely in their weedless conditions and green freshness to the eyes, but anything but agreeable to the olfactory nerves. Arrived at the gate a guard-house with outbuildings is seen on the left on the Portuguese side with soldiers. The gate itself is a large arched one with 6 stone tablets let in, bearing different dates such as 22nd August 1849, 22nd August 1870 and 31st October 1871. The remains of an old wall is seen on each side of the gate, though not now continuous. The cause of the Barrier Wall being made in A. D. 1573 was, so it was stated, for the protection of the country (China) and to prevent Chinese children from being kidnapped. A few Chinese soldiers and an officer guarded the door of communications, which was called by the Portuguese Porta do Cerco, so that no stranger might pass the boundary. At first the door was only opened twice a month, then every fifth day for the purpose of selling provisions; after that it opened at daylight . The tables are now turned; for this old gate was destroyed in some of the wars and the present gate is a large foreign structure with a guard house of Portuguese at it.

Beyond the Barrier there appears to be a piece of neutral ground. The distinction between occidentalism and orientalism; between civilisation and barbarism; between the European and the Asiatic is noticeable at once : for the well-made Portuguese road is at once changed for the wretched little foot path, meandering hither and thither. rugged and uneven never, properly made, unkept and uncared for, running through a perfect necropolis of poorer graves; or, at the very best, irregularly paved with long granite slabs unevenly laid and further allowed to sink to all angles.

The Praia Grande

One of the most enchanting scenes in Macao is that of this beautiful bay, quiet and graceful sweep of sea wall and rows of houses rising up the gentle slopes and the ancient forts and modern public buildings dotted here and there, while behind all rise the Mountains of Lappa and to the right those beyond the Barrier. All descriptions are imperfect; some fail from an attempt to liken this beautiful little gem with another world-renowned spot, the Bay of Naples. Let it be acknowledged at once that each is *sui generis* and attempt no comparison. There is no doubt when coming in from sea towards Naples and trying to detect Macao in Naples one does see a faint resemblence in one of the house-clad hills of the latter to Macao's central portion; but rather let one be content with enjoying the beauties of each and attempt no belittling of the grand proportions of the one or try to greaten the sweet gem-like curves and colours of dear old Macao. As an instance of what the artistic eye finds in the latter we quote from a short account of Macao

appearing in the "Dublin University Magazine" for
1848 :—

"A view of Macao from the sea is exquisitely fine. The
semicircular appearance of the shore, which is unencumber-
ed and unbroken by wharfs or piers [there are one or two
small landing places projecting] and upon which the surge
in continually breaking and receding in waves of foam,
whereon the sun glitters in thousands of sparling beams,
presents a scene of incomparable beauty. The Parade
[Praia Grande] which is faced with an embankment of stone,
fronts the sea and is about half a mile in length. A row of
houses of a large description extends along its length, * * *
Some are coloured pink, some pale yellow and others whit.e
The houses, with their large windows ,extending to the
ground * * * with curtains. * * convey an idea to the
visitor that he has entered a European rather than an
Asiatic seaport. This idea becomes still stronger by the
constant ringing of the church bells and passing and repass-
ing of * * priests clad in cassocks and three-cornered
hats. But this illusion is quickly dispelled when the eye,
turning towards the sea beholds the mumerous sampans and
mat-sail boats * * *, or glancing shorewards rests upon
figures clad in Chinese costume."

Unfortunately the outer Harbour on which the Praya
Grande faces is shallow and any large vessels which may
call at Macao have to lie some miles from the shore in the
offing. The Inner Harbour lying between the Peninsula
and the Island of Lappa affords a secure harbour, but, unfortunately it has been silting up with mud for many
years past. Of late years, however, a dredger has improved
matters. The Praya on the Inner Harbour presents a
great contrast to the other Praya for whereas quiet reigns
on the seaward one, the inland one is all bustle; rows of
Chinese vessels are anchored off the shore and boats and
sampans line the banks on which coolies are busy loading
or unloading cargo to carry into the stores, shops, and
wholesale Chinese merchants' places of business on this
Menduia Praya or into the back streets.

The Streets

To those interested in watching the life of the oriental
brought into sanitary order the busy streets of the Chinese

town will afford walks which will engage all their attention, while the quainter, quieter, lanes, alleys, tiny squares and larger Plazas will give a piquancy and zest and afford a striking contrast to the bustle of the business quarters.

" The exceedingly narrow and tortuous formation of the streets gives considerable pleasure to a ramble through Macao, shades away the sun when it is not at 90 degrees and reminds you of pictures you have seen of old Spanish and German towns."

In contrast with these narrow and tortuous old streets are the newer roads and the boulevard recently formed on what used to be the Campo without the City walls and below the Guia Fort and light house. Here rows of trees have been planted, chunam or cemented walks made under or between them with beds of flowers and a bandstand where a military band discourses fine music once or twice a week.

Of late years Macao after a period of stagnation has been much improved by new roads laid out over the Campo and about the hills. A grand new avenue to cost $ 300,000—and to lead in direct line from the Inner Harbour opposite the Steamboat Company's wharf to the Praya Grande, was mooted some years since; but the money has been spent on other improvements.

Camoen's Grotto

It is situated in the Casa Gardens which are entered by a gateway in the corner of the Plaza de Camoens. On entering, a small garden is seen in front of a large house; but bearing off to the right instead of going to the house and descending some steps one enters a large garden with many broad paths leading in different directions under umbrageous trees, while many ferns grow in the rocks, great masses of which are piled about in certain parts in nature's wild confusion. The garden until recently was private property but a few years sime the Portuguese Government bought it from its owner for $35,000. Since its purchase a band-stand has been erected and a fountain put up, the paths recemented (though they still retain their slipperyness as in other days) and ornamental walks and vases and borders made at certain places of little cubes or chips of white and red stone which have a somewhat bright and pleasing effect. Fortunately the Government has had the good taste not to carry this ornamentation to too great an extent and many parts of the garden are delicious in their wild condition. In one on two places, especially in one corner of the garden, gigantic boulders are piled one on the top of the other and a banian is perched on the topmost, while it sends its roots down in a perfect network over the masses of rocks on their way to mother earth, for the sustenance which the unique position of the tree prevents it from absorbing otherwise. On one of the mass of rocks thrown together in wild confusion was a small terrace where one might sit and view the landscape o'er. A flight of steps led up to it; but it has now been removed. A circular building with a slit through its roof at one side of the garden overlooking Inner Harbour will also attract attention. It was built for Laperouse and in it the scientific officers of his squadron, the *Astrolabe* and *Boussole*, made astronomical observations during the stay of those vessels in the Taipa in January 1787.

But the chief object of interest in the garden is the spot where the immortal Portuguese poet Luis de Camoens is said to have sat while composing part of his great epic poem the Lusiads. The retreat of the poet is not a cave, in the common acceptation of the term. On the surface of a gentle sloping hill, and between two large rocks, which seem to have been originally one, but now sundered a few feet apart by some one of nature's freeks, is the spot where Pontugal's noblest poet used to sit. Above the cleft rocks, and on them rests a mass of granite, which served the poet as a covert from the noonday's sun and stormy winds. He probably wrote the last three Cantos of the Luciads here.

With a laudable desire to restore this favourite retreat of their finest poet, to as near as possible like he left it, the Portuguese have removed a small quadrangular building in the Chinese style of architecture which crowned the mass of granite "resting above the cleft rocks" and which "commanded a fine view of the surrounding country. Towards east you behold the sea and the blue outlines of Lantao and other islands. Southward and westward you view the Taipa and Inner Harbour * * and various native craft. To the north is the Barrier, which forms a line of demarcation between the foreigners and celestials, and beyond it Tseen Shan or Casa Branca, a small walled town and military post" and Chinese customs station, "and behind which stretching away in the distance, is a meandering river and innumerable inlets," and nearer at hand Green Island, Ilha Verde, well worthy of its name. "The scenery altogether is romantic and charming." "The retreat of Camoens, at present wears altogether a different aspect to what it did in the days when the "poet hallowed the spot." The niche between the rocks "the identical spot where Camoens sat" "is decorated with a bronze bust of the poet, upon the base of which, in letters of bold relief, are records of his birth and death;" as follows:—

LUZ DE CAMOES

Neisceo 1524. Morreo 1580.

The bust bears evidence, were none other wanting, that be was handsome, of fine form, with eyes glowing full of life".

A number of upright granite slabs are either in the grotto itself or ranged in a row outside it, bearing some of them Cantoes from the famous Lusiads while others contain laudatory poems by different individuals.

This spot renders Macao "classic ground". A short account of Camoens may be here interesting. He was the most renowned of the Portuguese poets "and possessed talents of no ordinary character * * He was born at Lisbon" .His life seemed full of misfortunes. He lost his father in early life and the greater part of his family property at the same time. His mother had him educated at the university of Corinbra. Returning to Lisbon he was unfortunate in love being banished in consequence from the court. He went then as a soldier in a Portuguese fleet

to Morocco where he lost one eye in a fight.   He went to the
East and settled after a while at Goa and was unjustly
banished to Macao where "he lived happily and contented-
ly" for five years receiving the appointment of "Provedor
dos Defunctos" somewhat equivalent to the Official Administrator.   He amassed a small fortune but lost it all in ship-
wreck only saving his poem which he held above his head
with one hand while he swam ashore with the other.   He
finally returned to Lisbon and his Lusiads were published in
1572.   The name of this "invaluable contribution to poetic
literature" is derived from Lusus, the Latin name of Portugal.   It celebrates the discovery of India and has been
translated into various languages, there being several trans-
lations in English and French, four into Spanish and two
into Italian.   It has also been translated into Latin and
Hebrew.

On his return to his native land after 16 years absence
his misfortunes still accompanied him.   He received a small
pension from the King, but he died in absolute want in a
hospital at Lisbon, the day of his death being unrecorded
and his very winding sheet being given out of charity for
his grave.   "No monument told the passing stranger of
his worth till fifteen years after his decease.   Now however
a splendid one perpetuates his memory".

On the different stone slabs about the poet's monument
are the following tributes to his genius by men of different
nationalities.

2nd Slab from left

Yo poeta tambien, tambien soldado,
Si bien no por la fama enaltecido;
Tambien de hondas passiones arrastrado
Tambien de hados adversos combatidos

En el altar a tu estro consagrado
Menos angusto a fe que merecido
Suspendo de mi amor esta memoria
Tributo exiguo de tan alta gloria.

Don Huiberto Garcia de Luenedo. 1869

3rd from left

Vasco le cui folici ardito antenno
In coutre al Sol che ue ripartaft giorus.
Spiegaric voie o ter cola ritorno
Dove ogli var che ai caderoacconuay

Non piu di to asuero near sostenrio
Quel che fece al leictope chraggo et sconno.
No che un bo l'aygie noi suo sorggiorne
Ne die piu vel subertro a coltro penue

Et hor quelta est calti et tuon Luigi
Lantte altro stoude al glorioso velo
Che i tuoi spaluiati logai auliar meu lungo

Ouda quela a qui statzu il nostro Polo
Et achi foruea incontra l'suoi vessigi
Per lui del corso tue la funa agginogo

Torgunto Tasso

On the 4th Slab

SONNET TO MACAO

Gem of the orient earth and open sea
Macao that in thy lap and on thy breast
Hast gathered beauties all the lovliest
When the sun smiles in his majesty

The very clouds that top each mountain crest
Seem to repose there, lingering lovingly
How full of grace the green cathayou tree
Bends to the breeze and now thy sands are prest

With gentle waves which ever and anon
Break their awakened furies on the shore
Were these the scenes that poet looked upon
Whose lyre though known to fame knew misery more

They have their glories and earth's diadems
Have naught so bright as genius gilded gems

Dr. Hourin (?)

Macao 30th July 1849

On the 5th Slab

"Oh gruto de Macao soidao querida
"Onde tao doces horas de tristeza
"Do sandado passaei! gruta benigna.

"Que escutaste meus languidos suspiros;
" Que ouniste minhas queixas namoradas,
"Oh fresqui dao amena, oh grato asylo

"Onde me far acoltar de aserbas magoas
"Onde amor, onde a patria me inspiraram
"Os mariosos sous e os sons terrivies

"Que hao de affrontar os tempos o a injustica;
" Tu guardaras no seio os meus queixumes,
" Que contaras as provindouras eras.

"Os segredos d'amor que me escutaste,
" E tu diras a ingratos Portuguezes
"Se portuguez ou fui, se amei a patria,

"Se alem d'ella e d'amor, por outro objecto
" Meu caracao bateu, lucton meu braco
" On modulon meu verso eternos Carmes

Viscoude D'Almeida Garrett

At the back on a slab let into the side of one of the supporting boulders is the following:—

Patane, lieu charmant et si cher au Poete,
Je n'oublierai jamais ton illustre retraite:
Ici Camoes, au bruit du flot retentissant
Mela l'accord plaintif de son luth gemissant
Au flambeau d'Apollon allumant son genie
Il chanta les heros de la Lusitanie;
Du Tage, a l'urne d'or, loin des bords paternels
De bellone il cueillet les lauriers immortels.
Malheureux exile cet emule d'Homere
Acheta son genie; au prix de sa misere.
Il posseda, du moins pour charmer ses douleurs,
Les baisers de l'Amour et les chants des neufs Soeurs.
Lusus et les Chinois honorent sa memoire
Le tems qui d'etruit tout agrandira sa gloire.
Moi que cheris ses vers, que pleurai ses malheurs,
J'aiuais a salmer ces bois inspirateurs
Je visitais cent fois cet humble et noble asyle;
Dans ta grotte ô Louis, mon coeur fut plus tranquille.
Agite plus que toi je fegas dans les champs
Et le monde et mon coeur l'envie et les tyrans

Au Grand Louis de famveus Portugais Domine castillane
Soldat, religieux, voyaeur et poele exil'e.
L'humble Louis de Rienzi Francais d'oiigine romaine
Voyageur, religeux, soldat et poete expatrie

30 Mars (some designs between here) 1827

On one of the stones is inscribed the following verses in Latin by Sir John Davis, Governor of HongKong.

In cavernam ubi
Camóëns
Opus egregnim composuisse fertur.

Hic, in remotis sol ubi rupibus
Fronnes per altas mollius incidit,
 Fervebnt in pulchram camoenam
 Ingenium Camooëntis ardens

Signnm poetæ marmore lucido
Spirabat olim, carminibus sacrum,
 Parvumque, quod vivens amavit,
 Effigie decorabat antrum;

Sed jam vetustas, aut manus impia
Prostravit, eheu! Triste silentium
 Regnare nunc solum videtur
 Per scopulos, virides et umbras!

At fama nobis restat—at inclytum,
Restat pöetae nomen—at ingeni
 Stat carmen exemplum perene,
 Ærea nec monumenta quaerit,

Sic usque Virtus vincit, ad ultimos
Perducta fines temporis, exitus,
 Redens sepulchrorum inanes,
 Mamoris et celerem ruinam
     J. F. Davis

Macaio 1831

A writer thus gives his impressions of these gardens:—

"The gardens of Camoëns, the Portuguese poet, are full of curious little surprises that would fill the heart of a child with joy, something attractive meets the eye at every turn, and the place is full of turns, at every one of which something appears which you were not expecting. Old trees with their roots in the open air spread like a network down the perpendicular face of a rock, cause you to start in wonder at the way in which the ramifications reticulate into each other". 'The gardens are a quaint old haunt'. "On the topmost watch-tower you have a view of the Inner Harbour and the hills beyond; all around you besides is foliage, and saving this view the privacy is complete. Close to the town, yet in effect far away from it, you can only at intervals hear the confused hum that floats from the large city at hand".

The Public Gardens

The author remembers the site of the Public Gardens as simply a grassy plot; but with all the improvements, which the Portuguese have loved to beautify their little Colony, it has been laid out for many years past in flower-beds with numerous paths, seats, a band-stand, fountain and an aviary. The gardens are at the city end of the Praya Grande and occupy a narrow strip of ground, but at the far end a piece of rising ground is taken in as well. The band plays here once a week on Thursday afternoons.

Public Offices etc.

The Governor's town residence is on the Praya Grande and is a fine building. One of the most striking features about the public buildings in Macao is the clean state in which they are kept, affording often a striking contrast to those in Hongkong: it is a pleasure to the eye to rest on the former. The Chinese even note the difference and animadvert on those in Hongkong. This building was bought from the Baron do Cercal.

About the centre of the Praya Grande is situated the building now occupied as Government Offices. It is one of the finest and largest buildings on the Praya Grande; and was for many years the residence of the Governors. Sr. Roza transferred his gubernatorial dwelling to the fine Cercal Palace, further along, which is now the Government House of Macao; and the Judicial Department and that of the Junta de Tazenda were moved into the former headquarters of the Governor. As sufficient space room for the department of the Procurator of Chinese Affairs was found in this same building, it was moved from its old office, a house belonging to the old convent of Santa Clara.

A guard is always on duty at the door of this building. Entering and passing through the Hall, you ascend the stairs. In front of you is the court (a small one) for Chinese litigation, while to the right of it is a large Court kept in a most clean and bright condition (forming a great

contrast to the dinginess and dirt of English Courts) where
the Supreme Court holds its sittings. There is a dais at
at one end with a row of chairs on it behind a table. The
peristyle in front of this building was added amongst other
improvements by orders of the Viscount de San Januario
when presiding over the destinies of this province.

The Post Office

On the Transfer of the Governor's residence to the Cercal
Palace the guard House at the side of the old building and
on the other side of the lane running down to the Praya
Grande was available and to the great convenience of the
public was utilised as a Post Office. It is a small one-
storied neat looking little building having a portico in front
supported by eight pillars. Previous to the governor-ship
of Sr. Roza, the Post Office was in the hands of private
individuals, but he organised the service and made it a
department of the Government. The letter-box is fastened
on the door by which one enters into the Hall where the
public may wait for the distribution of letters. The back
part of the building is partioned off with glass and forms a
small room where the mails are sorted, the addressees of
letters having an opportunity of seeing the whole process
while waiting in the Hall for their letters.

There are several letter boxes about the town as well.
Part of the same building occupied by the Post Office is
used as a Government Telegraph Office.

There is a Telegraphic and telephonic connection between
Macao and Taipa.

It may be as well to mention here that the Eastern Extension Australasia and China Telegraph Co. have an
office in a large building, in one of the inner streets, on the
gradual slope rising to the Penha Hills; and messages may
be sent hence to any part of the world.

The Senate House

The Leal Senado, or Senate House, is a very old building
though over the front door the date 1876 appears.

Entering one finds oneself in an oblong room or hall with a door leading to a flight of steps and over this door is the following inscription in three lines:—

Cidade Do Nome De Deus, Nao Ha Outra Mais Leal

En Nome D'el Rei Nosso Senhor Dom Joao IV Mandou o Capitao Geral d'esta praça Joao de Souza

Pereira por este Etreiro em fè da muita le aldade, que Conheçu nos cidada d'ella em 1654.

This building is that in which the Government hold their sessions: it is two stories high; its base of granite, the rest of brick and mortar so also are the pilasters. The entablatuer rests on columns and the cornice is ornamented with green glazed vases. This spacious fabric was erected in 1784 and cost the sum of 80,000 taels. On the ground floor are the offices of the Director of Public Works. Going up the stone steps we find on our right hand over a door, Secretarix da Camara, i.e. Secretariat of the Municipal Council. Should our polite request to inspect the building be granted, we shall find two very old large paintings in the first office: one representing Macao in the olden days; and one the beheading of Christian martyrs in Japan. We next pass into two large rooms—the Council Rooms. A dais, under a red canopy, is at the end of the principal one with the Portuguese coat of arms supported by two angels and a panel of carved and gilded wood-work is below. A small room doing duty as a chapel opens off this, consecrated to our Lady of Conception, in which the members of the Senate hear mass before business. The Council Room has a number of old fashioned antique chairs in it with red cushions, the curtains are also red. There are a number of old paintings representing Portuguese royalty. The Outer Council Room has likewise paintings of the Governors of Macao hung round it.

On the left hand side of the stairs is the office of the Admimstraçao do Concellio. In the ante room to this are some very old-fashioned leather chairs.

Markets.

There are several markets in Macao, the San Domingos being the only important one. Here we may remark that many of the daily commodities of life are monopolies in Macao, the exclusive right to import and export kerosene was granted by tender in 1894 (to the highest bidder) for $3100 per annum. The late salt farmer obtaining it in 1897 for $3,000: and in 1899 for $17,000: there was also a gunpowder monopoly and a rickshaw one.

Churches, etc.

One of the most imposing structures in Macao is the ruined facade of the Jesuit Church of San Paulo which is visible from almost every point of the compass. The church was burnt on January 26th or 27th 1834 (or 1835?) A private manuscript states that Francis Peres and a few Jesuits in 1565 had a house in Macao where those of their Society used to lodge on way via Macao to Japan. The church which was erected by the Jesuits on their arrival in this part of China was accidentally destroyed by fire and was a noble building,–noble indeed it must have been if the rest of the structure was in keeping with the grand and picturesque hoary ruin left. This Collegiate church was erected in 1662 as expressed by an inscription engraved on a stone fixed in the western corner of the building:

Vrgini Magna Matri,

Civias Macaensis Lubens,

Posuit an. 1662.

The Church was consecrated to 'Nossa Senhora da madre de Deos' like its predecessor (built circa 1565). We cull the following description of it from an old work on Macao:—

'The frontispiece all of granite, is particularly beautiful. The ingenious artist had contrived to enliven Grecian architecture by devotional objects. In the middle of the ten pillars of Ionic order, are three doors, leading to the temple; then range ten pillars of Corinthian order, which constitute five separate niches. In the middle one above the principal door we perceive a human figure, trampling on the globe,

the emblem of human patriotism, and underneath we read
Mater Dei. On each side of the Queen of Heaven, in distinct places, are four statues of Jesuit Saints. In the
Superior division St. Paul is represented, and also a dove,
the emblem of the Holy Ghost. In this edifice is a clock,
which strikes quarters and hours, and to judge from an inscription on the principal wheel, Louis XIV made a present
of it to the Jesuit college'.

This splendid facade is nearly intact though slightly tou-
ched by the demolishing hand of time, and this though
hundreds of storms and typhoons must have assailed it
from every quarter of the compass during nearly three centuries and three quarters. The site of the church, only some
walls being left to mark its position, has been used as
a cemetery, though unused for some time now. A long
flight of steps leads up to it; this flight contains 130 steps
of granite of a width of from 60 to 80 feet. This church
was formerly the Cathedral; standing thus on a height under the walls of the Monte Fort it must have been even a
more conspicuous land mark than the present Cathedral.
There are stories current of subterranean passages leading
from St. Paul to Green Island which was formerly owned
by the Jesuits. In 1838 the side walls, though of great
thickness, were considered unsafe and were cut down to a
height of 22 feet; the facade, which is the most striking
object in the view of Macao from the harbour, was left
standing. This church took 8 years to build (1594-1602)
the Jesuits who erected it had early settled at Macao and
their followers provided the funds to purchase a house next
to this church; and in this house the Chinese were instruc-
ted and Portuguese educated. Even before 1594 this was
converted into an extensive Seminary of St. Paul and
in it often more than 'children of the inhabitants' were
taught the rudiments of learning A "College was afterwards
founded. It had two classes for Latin, two chairs for
theology, one for philosophy, and one for belles lettres.
The circuit of the Seminary contained a large hall for the
library, one for astronomical purposes, and an apothecary's
shop. Missionaries going and coming were lodged in the

Seminary which could accommodate 70 or 80 individuals.
This celebrated seat of learning (and of political influence)
in the East was broken up (1762) by order of Joseph I.
king of Portugal, and their members dispersed."

It appears that the church of St. Paul itself was entirely
built by Portuguese and Japanese, the latter probably being
converts exiled on account of their profession of Roman
Catholicism. Chinese are not mentioned, as at that date in
Macao's history the Chinese were not employed by the
Portuguese and were only permitted to sell provisions during the day in Macao and having to leave the City at night.
Vaults credited with containing treasure (for the Jesuits
had gathered much wealth together and were forced to
leave Macao with nothing but their breviaries) are, it is
stated, known to be under the long flight of stone steps in
front of the facade. And one writer affirms that not only
subterranean passages lead under water a considerable
distance to Green Island or Priests Island, but also up to
the Guia Fort.

THE CATHEDRAL

which is also a conspicuous object from many parts of
the City is a large building with two towers; one containing
a clock with two faces, the other a peel of three bells and a
small one. It has a ceiling of wood, pulpit and six con-
fessionals, old wood stalls and a curious old organ, a large
one being in the gallery above the main entrance. In one
of the rooms or passages at the back is an old painting of
the crucifixion of twenty-three Roman Catholic saints in
Japan in the 16th Century at Nagasaki. Two old red
leather chairs, like those in the Senate House, are placed
for the Governor and the Judge, with red stools. A picture
of St. John the Baptist preaching is more real than many
of the pictures in Roman Catholic churches. The Cathedral is dedicated to St. Peter. The principal district in
Macao derives its name from the Cathedral and is known
as the Bairo da Se. It is built on the high ground rising
behind the centre of the Praia Grande.

St Lawrence

The next largest district in the City is called *Bairo de St. Lourenco.* This church of San Lourenco, it is stated, may have been rebuilt in A. D. 1618. and within the last few years again as the roof fell in a few years ago. It is a large church, with broad stone steps leading up to it, being on a higher level than the road below. A picture of the saint is behind the high altar with a crown and dove descending from heaven on him. Two madonnas, with swords sticking in their breasts, and other images and altars abound. There are two towers to it: one containing a clock and the other a peel of three bells.

San Antonio

This smaller church is on the Square of Luiz Camoëns, opposite to the entrance to Camoëns' Gardens. It was burned down in 1809 and rebuilt by contributions. It contains the painting of a martyr saint bound with cords and shot at with arrows, which is worthy of a longer glance than the most of the paintings in the Macao churches deserve.

St. Joseph

One of the nicest churches in Macao is that of San Jose attached to the College of that mame. Though built many years before that date the Jesuits to whom it belongs, had not the pleasure of hearing mass in it before A. D. 1758. Architecturally, the proportions of the building are harmonious. The cupola is pierced with small, stained-glass windows, light is also admitted from the front, while other stained glass windows are to be found in the building. In one of the towers is a chime of six bells with an apparatus to work them consisting of a number of wooden handles (in a framework of wood) and attached to the bells by a system of rattan strings. A painting of St. Francis Xavier, apparently on his deathbed, is in this church as well as several mural tablets, amongst them that of Gonsalves, who was a Professor in the College, as well as a Chinese scholar. His tombstone consists of a long black slab let into the wall on on the left-hand side, beyond the entrance from the front door. It bears the following inscription:—

Hic jacet Rever. D. Joaquimus Alfonsus Gonsalves Lucitanus Presbyer Congregationis Missionis in regali Sancti Josephi Maconensi Collegio Professor eximus Regalis Societatis Asiaticæ solius extex Pro sinensibus missionibus solicitus petrutitia opera amico lusitano Lationque sermone composuit et in lucem alidit moribus suavissimo doctrina Præstanti integra vitaque plenus diebus in Domino quievit sexagenario Major quinto nonas Octobris anno MDCCCXLI. In memoriam tanti viri equs amici litteraturæque cultores Hunc lapidem consecravere.

Exit can be had to the roof of the church where a fine view of the city and its surroundings can be obtained:— From the cupola standing on the roof, one sees the front of San Paulo, the Monte Fort, the forts of Donna Maria II and Monha, Camoëns' Gardens, the hills beyond the Barrier, the Inner Harbour, Barracks, the Penha Hills, Taipa, and other islands. On a clear day the sea seems, beyond the Roads, almost locked in with islands; near and in the distance they lie blue on the horizon,

In the playground of the College, which is at the side of the church, are two large banyans, one of Falstaffian proportions. A stone seat runs all round it, at one or two points nearly touching the tree. This seat is about fifty or sixty feet in circumference. It takes twenty boys, joining hands, to form a circle round this ancient giant. On one of the author's visits to this spot he and six of his friends tried to form a ring round this tree, but it would have taken four more men to complete it.

In this connection it may be as well to give a short account of St. Joseph's College, the Jesuit clerical educational establishment, to which this church is attached.

This college, the Royal College of St. Joseph, has been termed the principal seat of learning in Macao. Founded by the Jesuits, at their expulsion in 1762, its activity ceased for twenty years when in 1784 the Court of Lisbon transferred this establishment to the "Congregation of Missions" and

in 1800 the charges to be paid by the Senate were definitely
settled. The priests belonging to this college are all European Portuguese, commonly six: their superior is appointed
from Europe. Of this institution, the principal aim is to
provide China with Evangelic teachers. Young Chinese, not
exceeding twelve in number, are admitted, and furnished
with what they necessarily want. If they evince a sincere
desire to become priests their education is directed that way;
but it generally requires ten years before the candidates
can receive the first order. Those whose vocation is dubious
wait longer or leave the college; others who want application,
or are noted for a misdemeanor, are sent away. The Professors give instructions in the Portuguese and Latin Gram-
mer, arithmetic, rhetoric, philosophy, theology, &c. Many
children of the inhabitants participate in them though few
of them are made priests. The Chinese language is taught
and English and French occasionally. Parents who can afford to pay for their children small monthly remuneration for
food and a cell (sic) fix them at the college, where the stu-
dents learn to speak genuine Portuguese, and acquire sometimes a taste for the improvement of their minds. Some
children dine at the college and join their families at night;
others attend the lectures delivered "gratis" by the Professors at distinct hours! So much for an old account of it.

The college contains a large number of class rooms and
spacious corridors. It is two stories high and has a basement as well. When the author visited it a few years since
there were seventy-five boys being trained to be priests,
thirty-three of whom were Chinese, the rest being Portuguese. There are two dormitories, each with twenty-five
beds, for the Portuguese boys, each boy having a bed to
himself. One dormitory serves for the Chinese. The college buildings are put up round three sides of a square and
on one of the verandahs there is a photographic studio.
The library, contained in a small room, has some 600 volumes in it, in Portuguese, Latin, and English, &c. The
old library was burned. There is a replica in the library
of the bust of Camoens. An old bell is hung up near a

flight of stairs bearing an inscription and the date 1719. In the sitting room in the college is a painting, by a Chinese probably, of Gonsalves with the following inscription:—

O Revdo. Pe. Joaquim Alfonso Gonsalves
da congregacao de S. Vincente de Paulo, insigne
sinologo Portuguez, nascao em Tojal aos de Marco
de 1781 e falleceu no Seminario de S Jose de Macau
dos 3 de Outubro de 1841.

The Bishop of Macao has a sitting room and bed-room on the top floor, and the servants have their quarters in the basement.

There is a printing office and book-binding place in the college. Books are printed and published here, and a weekly religious newspaper issued.

HERMITAGE OF PENHA

Though the city his now grown up to this small church yet when it was first erected it was so far out in the country as to merit the name of hermitage. An old writer thus describes it:—

"On the western hill, denominated Nillau, the Augustine friars began (1662) the Hermitage of Penha—'ermida de nossa Senhora da Penha de Franca'—devotees enlarged it in 1624. Portuguese ships going into the harbour are accustomed to salute the hermitage with a few guns. Its revenue depends upon the liberality of individuals and on promises sea-faring people occasionally make in an hour of distress, to acknowledge by gratuities the favour which they think the Virgin Mary bestowed upon them, in preserving their lives and property".

The view from this church is very fine, forming a counterpart of that from the Mongha fort, while yet many features not visible from that vantage point come into view from this. The whole city lies spread out before our feet. In the distance the hills in Chinese territory with the graceful sweep of the Barrier isthmus and the old gateway, a trifle nearer rises the Mongha Fort, then in the mid-distance the square old Monte Fort, covering the top of the

hill it is placed on, and cutting out of view the valley and
the Campo which lie behind it. Then a dip in the hills,
which rise again, crowned by the Guia Lighthouse and its
encircling fort, while the ground appears to fall towards the
sea at the extreme end of the Praya, the Gap being hidden
by the hills, capped by the ruined fort (which has lately
being repaired) beneath which stands the Military Hospital;
next come the San Francisco Barracks and Fort of San
Francisco and the neat little Gremio down on the Praya.
Then the beautiful curve of Praya Grande itself, which ends
at the Bom Parto Fort, nearly below us, but a little to the
right. Behind the Praya the ground rises again and a
ruined garden enclosed in stone walls is below us. The
Cathedral, some distance off, is a prominent object though
by no means picturesque, the ruined portico of San Paulo
forming a much more pleasing subject for the eye to rest
on. This is to the left of the Monte. Still somewhat
distant, and somewhat to the left, is the green grove which
we know to be Camoens' Garden and the muddy waters
of the Inner Harbour are still further to that side, broaden-
ing out in the distance with a panorama of hills as a
background. Its hither shores are lined by the Chinese
quarters of the town. In the mid-view rises St. Joseph
with its cupola and further off San Lorenzo is seen.

There are a number of other churches in Macao, but none
that call for any special mention. They are San Lazaro,
Santa Clara, in connection with the old Convent of that
name, San Agostino, opposite the theatre and San Domingos which is near the entrance to the square at the opposite
end of which is the Senate House. The facade of this is
distinctly Iberian in character.

There is a small chapel in the Guia Fort—the 'ermida da
nossa senhora da Guia, or Neves'.

The English Church

The English church is in the Plaza do Luiz Camoëns
No. 11, next the entrance to Camoëns' Gardens. It is a
small chapel, seating about forty persons. There are two

mural tablets: one to the memory of Mr. Endicott and one
to Mr. H. D. Margesson. Below the church at the back is
the old Protestant Cemetery. Here lie the remains of
many who were well known in the early days of English
intercourse with China. Amongst the graves may be
noticed those of the Rev. Robert Morrison, D. D., F. R. S.,
first Protestant missionary to China, who arrived in that
land in 1807, and who founded the Anglo-Chinese College
in Malacca, an institution which did much good in its day.
He likewise made the first translation of the Bible into
Chinese, prepared a Chinese-English Dictionary and other
works. He was also employed as a translator by the Hon-
ourable East India Company and after living a quarter of a
century in the East, died in Canton in 1834. The grave of
George Chinnery, the painter, who lived many years in
Macao, is to be noted; and those of the English Admiral.
Sir Philip le Fleming Senhouse, who died at Hongkong in
1841, and from whom Mount Senhouse, on Lamma Island.
near Hongkong, is named. Also that of the Right Honour-
able Lord Henry Churchill, Captain of H. M. S. "Druid".
fifth son of the late Duke of Marlborough. Also the grave
of J. R. Morrison, a distinguished Interpreter in the early
days of European intercourse with China.

The New Protestant Cemetery is out near the Barrier.
near to Bella Vista. On the slopes of Bella Vista are some
old English graves, one being that of an infant son of Dr.
Morrison. Time has worn off most of the inscriptions.
(One or two old graves of former English residents are to
be found in Camoëns' Garden.) There are eleven of these
old tombstones, belonging to the century before last and
the first half of last century. There are graves of Protestant English and Germans, who were not allowed to be
buried within the precincts of the Holy City. The hill was
then called the Meersberg.

Chinese Temples

There is one Chinese temple within and three without the
limits of the city. In short there are several of them about

Macao. and worthy of a visit by the curious.

THE AMACAO TEMPLE

The temple near the inner harbour is remarkable for its situation. A mass of gigantic boulders are heaped together by Nature in chaotic confusion and at their feet are the main buildings of the temple while stone steps lead up amongst the masses of the rock, amidst which here and there, are perched different buildings and shrines. Inscriptions are cut in the rocks, and stone seats are placed on the little terraces, which occupy every coin of advantage, grudgingly granted by the great granite boulders.

In the main building of the temple is a very good model of a Chinese junk with wooden anchors, &c., complete. The goddess came from Foochow to Macao in the junk of which this is a model, after various oppositions made to her departure. One of the signs that she should go was the falling ill of all the sailors with colic. The sword of a large swordfish is also preserved in this temple as a thank-offering presented by a fishing-junk for a fruitful season in fishing. This temple which is known as the Amacao Temple, or that of 'The Lady of the Celestial Chambers', had its beginning about A. D. 1573, when a Fukienese ship becoming unmanageable at sea, all perished but one sailor, a devotee of the goddess, Matsopo, who embracing her sacred image with the determination to cling to it was rewarded by her powerful protection, according to his own belief, and preserved from perishing. The ship, driven through the storm, weathered it, and the devoted sailor landed at Macao and built on this spot a temple at the hillock of Amako, as being the best situation he could find for the only temple to his patron saint which his slender means would permit of his erecting.

Fifty years after an lmperial Messenger in the course of a dream had the locality of a lake, containing many and valuable pearls revealed to him by the goddess, and in grateful acknowledgement of the great favour thus granted him, he built a temple on the spot to her.

The origin of the present congeries of buildings was due to

Fukienese and Tiuchiu merchants subscribing 7000 taels to build some more fitting shrines for the favourite object of their worship. The upper temple is dedicated to the Goddess of Mercy; the middle one is styled The Temple of Universal Benevolence; while the lower one is named Amako.

THE MONGHA TEMPLE.

This is a historically interesting spot, as here the first treaty between the United States and China was signed on the 3rd of July 1844; and also here in 1849 the head and arm of Governor Amaral were hidden in ashes, after he had been massacred at the Barrier by the Chinese. This temple is at a little distance along the lane that is at the back of the New Protestant Cemetery. It has a blank wall at each side. Entering the garden, one finds oneself in a large open space, behind which are the several buildings composing the temple. In these buildings are to be found the Three Precious Buddhas, a goddess riding on an elephant and other idols. Chinese frescoes, some in relief, adorn the place: one of them representing The Fat Buddha with a pack of boys playing with and teasing him, though such a god, the personification of good-nature, is evidently too good-natured to be teased. A garden is attached to the place, and in it there is some curiously ornamented tiling, the figures, &c., being in high relief; but which is, however in rather a dilapidated condition.

MA KAU TEMPLE

Under the curious little fort of Donna Maria II, a rocky point runs out into the sea, and just above the rocks is a very small temple to the Goddess of Heaven. It depends for its revenue partly on a tax on fishing-boats, which it levies, but the silting up of the water in the bays has caused this revenue to decrease of late years: the temple is one that has been in existence for some hundreds of years.

It is from these rocks, the Ma Kau Rocks, that Macao takes its name. A path leads down to the temple from the road.

Forts

There was enmity between the Dutch and the Portuguese and for this, and probably other reasons, Macao, being an open, unprotected place, it was resolved to wall and fortify it. In 1607 it seems to have had no such defences: the Monte Fort was built in A. D. 1675. The Monte Fort, or Fortaleza do Monte de St. Paulo, is a conspicuous object, viewed from almost every part of Macao. It is a large square fort covering the whole of the top of a large hill, which rises with gradual slopes and occupies, roughly speaking, the centre of the peninsula. It is a spot of considerable historical interest, coming often into notice in the earlier records of the settlement. It was from this fort that the shot was fired which killed the leader of the Dutch when they landed at Caçilha's Bay and were marching along the Campo to take the City. The place where the Dutch admiral fell is now marked by a monument. There are a number of buildings inside the walls of this old fort, some of which serve as a prison. A polite request will secure permission from the officer in charge to enter. A climb up to this fort (though the lanes and alleys one passes are narrow and the houses of the humbler class), will repay one by the extensive view which one obtains of this picturesque Portuguese Colony. The City lies below one's feet, to the left the Barracks, Fort of San Fransco, the Military Hospital, the old tiny fort of San Joao, recently rebuilt, and the ancient grey wall of the City which leads from this Monte Fort down the hill and rises up on the other side to the old fort and then goes down the hill again towards the Praya. There is the cupola of San Jose, and beyond it the Penha Hills. The islands in the Inner Harbour from this point look different. One sees the Campo, the Guia, Monga, Donna Maria Segonda Forts, the Church and Cemetery of San Michael, the Barrier, Green Island, The Chinese Territory, Camöens' Gardens, the Cathedral, the Chinese town and gardens are all visible; but it is well nigh impossible to enumerate all the objects to be seen from this vantage ground; for a walk round the ramparts of this fort presents a varying panorama and most of the objects of interest come in view, one after the other, as the spectator's standpoint changes.

THE MONGA FORT

The Monga is a small square fort, placed on the higher one of two rocky hills overlooking the peninsula. A broad. but almost disused road, leads up to it from the gate of The New Protestant Cemetery. It is well worth an ascent, as the view is very fine and a fresh breeze is often blowing. Arrived at the fort, to the north lies the large gate of the Barrier, with the road running along the middle of the isthmus to it and through it to Chinese territory. Beyond lie some lower hills, while a ridge of higher heights shuts out further view of what used to be an unapproachable land. This ridge is called by the Chinese, Pak Shan Leng, The Northen Hills. Turning towards the south, the whole peninsula lies spread out below one's feet. To our right are the muddy waters of the Inner Harbour with its comparatively narrow neck opening out into a wide bay-like expanse, Green Island in its centre, and the river coming down into it in the distance. At our feet a large level plain spreads itself out,—well-cultivated vegetable-gardens, intersected by one or two roads, Chinese hovels. and hamlets lie in different places on its edges. The green little knowl and umbrageous trees, amidst which is nestled Camoëns' Grotto, forms a pleasant background to the mass of Chinese roofs, while it itself is nearly surrounded by hills, thus giving a pleasing variety to the view. The Monte Fort shuts out a sight of the Praya, but in the distance to the right is seen the Penha Hills and the old grey City wall rises first to the Monte then down and up again to the little old fort and again down, this fort of San Paolo and part of the City are also seen, A peep of the Outer Harbour shows between the Monte Fort and the hill, on the brow of which stands the Military Hospital, portion of which is in the line of view and so are also the Gap and the height above it, on which the lighthouse and the Guia Fort rear themselves. This range of hills continues till it sinks into Caçilha's Bay, rising again with a hill to support the Fort of Donna Maria II, while the ornamented Bella Vista is closer at hand, and still further beyond the hills fall into lower heights and run out in a long tongue which terminates in masses of rock, washed and beaten and hollowed out by the dashing waves of centuries of the restless ocean. This rocky portion is called Macao Rock and there is a temple here. Beyond lies the sea with islands and islets, fretted with silver foam when the wind roars and raves in its mad glee. Towards the East are the Nine Islands and the lofty, abrupt top of Lantao which now is British, rises to the height of 3050 feet.

BAR FORT

The Bar Fort, or Fortaleza de Santiago is at the entrance to the Inner Harbour. It is built on the lower slope of the hill at the water's edge. The soldiers have tastefully laid out several flower beds in it. There is also a chapel dedicated to the patron saint, who appears life-sized and armed with sword and shield and in warlike dress.

FORTE DE D. MARIA

From this fortress which overlooks Caçilha's Bay, the view is also very fine; but considerably different in its character from that seen from Monga Fort; though many of the same objects appear, yet viewed from a different standpoint, the panorama spread out before one's eyes from the different heights in Macao present considerable differences. The outlook from this height is more of the country and the sea, as some of the hills now hide the greater portion of the dwellings. The fort itself is a curious little place, a drawbridge carries one over the dry moat at the gate which is arrived at, after ascending a zig-zig path. A well of delicious cold water is within the walls of the fort. From this spot are seen Camoëns' Gardens, the Monte Fort, the Inner Harbour and the large hills on the opposite side with Caçilha's Bay lying below.

THE GUIA FORT

The Guia Fort is one of the most conspicuous objects in a

landscape where nearly very thing seems conspicuous. It crowns the Guia Hill and is approached by a zig-zag path from the Gap. Within its enclosures is an old chapel, containing old graves and opened once a year when a procession ascends to it. The lighthouse is also within the walls of this fort. The light is a revolving one going by clockwork, the works being wound up by two convicts, who have a cell for their incarceraton within the fort. The Guia Fort was built in A. D. 1637 and the lighthouse in 1865.

FORTS OF SAN FRANCISCO, BOM PARTO AND ST. PETER

The Praya Grand is bounded by two forts and had a little fort, that of St. Peter, in the middle. The two other forts are one at each end of the Praya. San Francisco, of grey stone, being just below the Barracks (several yellow buildings, through which entrance into it is effected) of that name and nearest the Guia Fort. In 1622 there was but one battery, 'the lower battery dates from 1632'.

The Bomparto Fort, Bartuarte de nossa Senhora de Bomparto, is at the far end of the Praya. It is, we believe, not used as a fort now, but serves as a residence for one of the military officers.

A city wall, already mentioned, ascends to the chapel on the top of the hill above it. An extension of the Praya Grande and the Praya Menduca (the Praya at the Inner Harbour) is contemplated from below this fort, round to the Bar Fort. The Bomparto Fort had three batteries. This fort is connected with the fort at Taipa Point, on one of the islands lying off the Outer Harbour, by a telegraph line, which lands at Bishop's Bay, a small sandy bay a little beyond the end of the Praya, below the Penha Hills. The end of the cable may be seen at low water and a soldier is here to guard it. The telegraph offices for this Government telegraph are at the fort, and signals can be exchanged with other places. There is a lay figure dressed in armour in this fort and, in one of these forts, there is an old bell bearing an inscription in Portuguese and the date 1707.

It will be found on visiting the forts in Macao that every

thing is most beautifully clean and neat and the soldiers and officers most polite and civil. Above Bishop's Bay were a number of dirty squatters' houses. These are being, or have been, cleared out for sanitary reasons.

Military Hospital

From forts it is an easy transition to the Military Hospital of San Janario, which, erected in 1873, is built on a most commanding and healthy site fronting the sea. It is on the slope of the hill, just below the old fort of San Joao and just above the San Francisco Barracks, being one of the first objects that the visitor to Macao sees from the deck of the steamer. It is named after the Viscount S. Januario, a former Governor of the Colony, during whose term of office it was built, the former military hospital being in the old Convent of San Augustino. The site was that of an old gunpowder manufactory. The model for the construction of the building was the Hospital of San Raphael in Belgium. It cost $38,500, and covers 75 metres by 34. The building consists of a main body facing the sea with several wings running back from it. In the front are the Entrance Hall, the porter's Lodge, the Quarters for the Chief Hospital Attendant and his Assistant, and the stairs to the Secretary's Office in the upper story. In the Northeast part there are apartments for the Physician, the Chaplain, a room containing surgical instruments, the Dispensary, and the Chapel, while in the South-west portion of the building there are Quarters for the Officers, Bath-rooms, and the Linen Stores. The upper storey contains the Committee Room, Secretary's Office, and the Director's Office. The wings contain Surgical and other wards for Sergeants and Reserved Ward, Accountant's Quarters, and a Hall for Surgical Operations, Cells, and Quarters for Military Servants.

The Mortuary, Room for Post Mortem Examinations and Room for the Collection of Soiled Linen are in a separate building some four or five metres distant from the main building and still further distant in the same direction is the Guard House. There is a garden to the South-west for the use of convalescents and there is also a tower for an Observatory.

St. Rafio, or Civil Hospital

This hospital, one of the ancient institutions, was erected by the Brotherhood of Mercy. Admission was by petition to the Provedor and both heathen and Christians were admitted, a wall dividing the male and female quarters.

The Leper Asylum

This is another of the ancient charitable institutions of Macao.

Santa Casa de Misericordia

As the font and origin of the charitable institutions of Macao, it will be interesting to quote an account of this parent association from an old writer on Macao:—

"Donna Leonara, consort of King John II, founded in Lisbon (1489) a Brotherhood of Mercy, known by the appellation of 'comfraris be nossa Senhora ba Misericordia,'—The foundation of the Santa Casa de Misericordia,—The Holy House of Mercy at Macao was laid in 1596 and its first Provisor,—"Provedor"—was Melchior Carneiro, Governor of the Bishoprick of Macao. To assist fellowmen, whose means of subsistence are too small and inadequate for the maintenance of a numerous family, to relieve bed-ridden, respectable people, and those who reluctantly go abroad asking for alms, and to bring up orphans and foundlings; these are the sacred duties which this worthy society profess to impose upon themselves. In any country where Portugal ever settled their thoughts were bent, it seems, upon forming benevolent institutions, like that we are alluding to. Reformed rules for its management were drawn up, (1617) and confirmed (1649) by John IV, who took the Santa Canta Casa de Misericordia under his immediate protection. In compliance with the "compromise" of 1627, the collective numbers nominate electors to choose a Provisor, Secretary and Treasurer, with the Deputies to form a Board of thirteen. The individuals thus selected are at liberty to decline the trust or to accept their respective charges for the period of

one year, ending on the 3rd of July. The Provisor may with
the concurrence of a majority of the Board, take certain
resolutions; but in fixed cases, such as in the election of new
members, a general meeting is required. The Board meets
twice a week, in a spacious hall not far from the fine church,
dedicated to our Lady of Mercy,—nossa Senhora da Misericordia. The members of this brotherhood do not contribute,
duty bound, to the formation of a productive fund; they
engage merely to act as trustees. On certain bulky articles
of trade one per cent. being added to the regular custom-
house duty, [There is no custom-house in Macao now, as
there was in the days when this was written as Macao is
now a free port,] half of its total amount is, at the end of
the year received by the Treasurer, the other half goes, as
alread mentioned, to the Monastery of St. Clare. In 1833
the receipts were 3806 taels; besides this stock, which
is, of course, subject to much fluctuation, the members of
the Board manage all those sums which living or deceased
persons may choose to throw into the coffers for purposes
fully explained in writing." This Holy House of Mercy
was abolished about thirty-five years ago; but was revived
again in 1832 when, as stated below, a lottery was first started. 'The old rules were revived and the sanction of the
authorities obtained'. Of late years a lottery has been
resorted to as a means of obtaining money. It was farmed
to a wealthy merchant, representing a Chinese syndicate
The proceeds were thus allotted:—54 per cent. in prizes of
different amounts and 25 per cent., less 8 per cent. paid to the
Santa Casa, went to the merchant. So that the main subsidy
now is the monthly one derived from the lottery. The funds
of the Santa Casa are invested in shares of Hongkong public
Companies. The institution is in a flourishing state, great
care, it is said, being exercised in the management of the
Society's money matters; and the institutions, such as the
San Raphael Hospital, mentioned above, the Asylums, and
others are also carefully managed.

THE CHINESE HOSPITAL

Copying the Christian practices of Western nations in

instituting hospitals for the sick, the wealthy Chinese, in
Hongkong, Canton, and Macao, as well as at some other
ports and cities, have within the last score or two of years
established charitable societies, having often a hospital in
connection with them. The one in Hongkong has had the
benefit of being under Government supervision (having
first been forced into existence by the Government) and for
some time past having doctors trained in Western science
connected with it. The same holds good with the Macao
Chinese Hospital, which is subjected to thorough Government inspection by the Portuguese authorities, who insist
on the place being kept in a clean and wholesome condition.
"A full account of all that transpires" is given to the
Portuguese Government physician, who has a frequent inspection of the hospital. The entrance to this hospital is
not very prepossessing, as a stone wall fronts one. A clean
Chinese attendant meets one and points the way to the inner departments, first of which to be seen is that devoted to
the idols. Instead of being venerable in dirt and cobwebs,
this temple apartment is clean, "the floors are scrupulously
white and not a bit of dirt is visible." A cup of tea is presented to the visitor, who then interviews the attendants,
amongst whom is seen a well-dressed doctor. The drug-
store is well-stocked with many of the herbal simples of the
Chinese pharmacopœa, nor amongst the materia medica are
wanting several well-known Western medicines; behind the
drug-store are seen a number of "benches arranged facing a
sunny out-look" on which the convalescents are seated. "A
stately flight of stone steps" and 'a promanade through a
carefully kept garden" lead to the various wards. "From
the open doors and ventilated roofs the patients can see
beautiful flowers and foliage and rest their weary eyes upon
one of the loveliest bits of landscape gardening in Macao".
Ventilation is ensured in each small apartment, both at the
side and at the top. Small comfortable beds are provided
for the patients and warm coverlets, which latter attract attention from their cleanliness. "A tiny tea-set, a bowl,
chop-sticks, and the other little table ornaments which the

Chinese seem to think necessary" are provided for each patient. Everything in this hospital is described as being clean, or clean and tidy, and this extends even to the kitchen itself, which in an average Chinese house is the dirtiest part of the dwelling. Disinfectants are freely used—the floors being washed twice a day, furniture, "and the beds are dusted with a wet cloth" once in that period, the bed-linen and towelling are changed daily, the patients also *mirabile dictu* having a bath once a day and a change of underclothing. The attendance given to the charity patients by the Chinese of the hospital is described as most tender and kind. "In some of the spaces were mildly insane patients, and it was noticeable that the attendants treated them with the utmost gentleness".

A Leper Hospital is kept up on the Island of Caho by the Government.

St. Clare, or Santa Clara

Mosteiro de Sa. Clara—This old convent is just behind the Public Gardens where an ancient gateway gives access to a long flight of stone steps leading up to the door of this former nunery. "A nun of Toledo by the name of Jeronyma de Ascencao chose China for her field of labour. She arrived at Manila (1621) with some nuns. Liberty was at last granted to her to go to Macao and there lay the foundation of a convent in honour of St. Clare. Jeronyma died and six nuns came to Macao with the Abbess Leonora de St. Francis in November 1633. Erected by voluntary contributions and alms of the faithful, the nuns took possession on the 30th. of April 1634. Convent was consumed by conflagration in 1825, but is now 1634 rebuilt." There were forty nuns in this convent; but it is now turned into a school. It is curious to go through the building with its large spacious rooms. When we visited it the Lady Superioress had not been outside its walls for twenty years. There is a chapel in connection with this convent.

Schools

There are a number of other educational institutions in

Macao besides those mentioned above. We have already spoken of St. Joseph's College or the Seminario de S. Jose, which has a long list of Professors, headed by a Rector and Director Esperitual, comprising in their number Instructors in Theology, Philosophy, Rhetoric, Natural History, Physics, Latin, Geography and History, French, English, Portuguese, Chinese, and Music.

THE CENTRAL SCHOOL AND OTHERS

The Escola Central is for Primary Instruction and has a number of masters. It is divided into three, a Higher, Middle, and Lower School. Instruction is aso given in Music, Gymnastics, Dancing, and Chinese in both Pekingese and Cantonese.

Near the end of the old City wall is a small building, the Escola Publica de Lingua Portugeza para China, for the instruction as the name shows, of Chinese in the Portuguese Language. It is presided over by one Professor or Master.

There is an association for the promotion of the instruction of Macaoese, consisting of a President, Secretary, Treasurer, and four members.

There is a Public School for Girls in the parish of Saint Lourenco, and one in the Cathedral parish. There are also one or two Public Schools for Boys.

Besides the above there is, or was, an Escola Commercial with an Englishman and Chinese as Professors. Amongst the schools may be mentioned the Italiae School, Asylo das Filhas de Caridade Canosimas, baving eight sisters as teachers with a Regenta as Head.

THE COLLEGE OF SANTA ROZA

This institution has its origin as an asylum for female orphans well-nigh two centuries ago. It is thus written of:—

"An institution of this kind was an early thought of the Brotherhood of Mercy; but no efficient means could be devised for its duration. A temporary foundation for thirty widows and orphans began in 1726; they were fed, and the orphans taught to manage a house. One of the most deserving of the inmates was annually endowed with the amount of one-half per cent. on the whole importation of trade, which the Senate had set apart for a nuptial portion; this half per cent. rose in 1726 to 406 taels; in 1728, to hardly 60 taels. From this epoch the institution remained suspended till in the year 1782 the Brotherhood made a proposition to establish a new one in conjunction with the Senate: the proposal was accepted. The Senate gave four thousand taels and the name of Asylum of Sta. Rosa de Lima,—Recolhimento de Santa Rosa de Lima. This stock increased by liberal gifts and legacies is lent at respondentia. The net proceeds of the premium, determines the number of girls who can be admitted. No one is received but with the consent of the Bishop, who appoints a priest (for there is a chapel in the house), an Inspector, and a woman of good repute, Regent of the Community. A school mistress teaches Religion, Reading, Writing, and Needlework. Female children, whose fathers can afford to pay a certain allowance for food, lodging, &c., are not refused admittance when places are vacant, and the Bishop does not start any objections. Orphans there educated, may with his consent, accept the situation of a teacher in any family, and the proposal of a matrimonial union (should a suitable match happen to be offered). In this event a portion is bestowed, but the amount depends on the resources and the good will of the Bishop."

The College of Santa Coza da Lima for Girls is now presided over by a Committee, consisting of the Bishop as President, a Vice-president, a Treasurer, and Secretary, and a couple of members. There are a number of Professors, English, French, Music, and Dancing being all included in the curiculum.

Artisan Training School

A school described as such was started in Macao "for the benefit of Macaoese orphans and sons of poor persons who are unable to provide for the higher education of their children. An annuity was necessary for the maintainance of the establishment in its different branches, but this is

fully provided for by subsidy from the Government and the
various charitable institutions of Macao".

As to the maintinance of some of these schools the Leal
Senado supports two free schools, a boys' and a girls'—The
Escola Central do Sexo Masculino and The Escola Central
do Sexo Feminino.

Besides these there are the Lyceum, maintained by
Government, the Senate contributing $4000 annually.

Clubs

The Club Unioao is presided over by a Committee, con-
siting of a President, Secretary, Treasurer, and two members. The habitat of the Club is or was, the pretty theatre
of Dom Pedro II. The spacious room in the centre which
serves as a theatre can be used as a ball-room, while the
smaller rooms in front serve as a reading-room, &c. A number of papers are to be found on the tables and a considerable number of books in the book-shelves.

The Gremio Militar is a military club on the Praya just
beyond the Public Gardens. It is a tasteful, pretty, little
building containing Reading Room, Card-rooms, &c, &c.,
The Committee is composed of a President, a Vice-President,
a Treasurer, a Secretary, and a Vice-Secretary. It appears
to have been somewhat enlarged of late years.

Tennis Club

The Tennis-Club is just behind the New Protestant Cemetery. It has two chunam Courts. Visitors are allowed to
join on application to the Secretary and payment of a
small monthly subscription.

Monuments

In what was the Campo behind the range of hills on
one point of which is the lighthouse, but which part of the
Campo is now taken into the boulevard-like garden, or
garden-like-boulevard, is a monument erected to the memory of the victory over the Dutch when Macao was attacked
by the latter "during the long-continued war in the East
between Portugal and Holland, the latter capturing many

of the Portuguese Colonies, such as Malacca, Point de Galle, &c. On June 22nd 1622, Admiral Ryersyoon with eighteen vessels appeared off Macao from Batavia. He landed a considerable force at Caçilha's Bay and advanced upon the City, but after an unavailing attempt to capture it, was obliged to retrace to his ships, leaving the Commander of the land force behind him. This officer was killed by a round shot from the Monte Fort." It was a disasterous defeat for the Dutch, the Portuguese fighting bravely.

The monument is a short, thick, octagonal, stone column, mounted on a stone base, surmounted by the Portuguese coat of arms, carved in stone also. The whole is surrounded by an iron railing with granite pillars. There are inscriptions on both front and back of the column in a scroll. In front is the following:—

Para perpetua na Memoria dos Vindouros
A Victoria que os Portuguezes de Macau
Por Intercessao do Bemaventurados. Joao Baptista
A quem Tomaram por padroeiro
Alcancaram
Sobre Oitocentos Hollandezes Armados
Que de Trese Naos de Guerra Capitaneados
Pelo Almirante Roggers
Desembarcaram na Praia de Cacilha
Para Tomarem esta Cidade
Do Santo Nome de Deus de Macau
Em 24 de Junho de 1622.

That on the back is as follows:—

No Mesmo Logar Oude
Uma Pequena Cruz de Pedra
Commemorava
A Accao Gloriosa dos Portuguezes
Mandou
O Leal Senado
Levantar este Monumento
No anno de 1864.

On the base in front is the date

de Marco
1871.

(The bust of Camoens has already been noticed in an account of the Gardens where his cave or grotto is to be found.) On the opposite side of the road from that on which the monument to the great Portuguese Victory is situated, but further away from the City, is a piece of ground laid out as a garden and having in its centre a statue to the late Count de Senna Fernandes, which was erected by some of the Chinese in the Colony. The statue of the Count is in official dress, and on the pedestal there are inscriptions in Portuguese and Chinese. The former is as follows:—

Para Perpetua a Memoria do Beneniseito
Cidadao
Bernandino de Senna Fernandez
Major Honorario
Commendador da Ordem Militer de
Nosso Senhor Jesus Christo
Commendador da Ordem de Elephante Branco
de Siam
Cacalleiro de Antica e Minto pobre Ordem
Da Torre e Espada, do Valor Lealdade e Merito
Fidaho Cavalleiro da Casa Real
Consul de Siam e da Italia
I Barao Viscounte e Conde de Senna Fernandez
A graciado Comamedalha de Frata
de Merito Philanthropia e Generosidade
Chevalier Sauveteurs des Alpes Maritimes
Socio Protettore de Associazioni dei
Benemeriti Italini
Muito Apreciado pela Communidade Chineza
de Macau
Pelo seu animo justiceiro e provada
Estima e sympathia
Aos negociantes Chinezes
A quem sempre Dispensava Proteccao
e Apoio

* * * * * * *

Esta Estatua foi Mandaro Erigir por
Lu-Cheo-Chi, Cham Hau-in, Ho-Liu-Vong,
e outros negociantes Chinezes de Macau
Em Testemunho de Amizade e Gratidao.

Fountains

There are several fountains, or hydrants, where the
water is supplied for public use. One or two of these are
rather pretty spots. Especially is (or perhaps was, as we
believe some alterations are in progress here) this the case
with the Fonte de Solidao. The "fonte" itself calls for no
especial notice, the water being simply conducted into a
trough; but a little to the left a flight of stone steps leads
up from the road and by going up and trending a little to
the right, one comes in a few steps to a pretty double grotto—a lovely little spot, hewn out of the solid rock, and
green with numbers of beautiful ferns, with water dripping
from the rock and trickling down over the greenery. This
"fonte" is on the land-side of the sea-side road leading from
the Gap to Caçilha's Bay.

Another of these places is behind the Padre's Gardens as
they used to be called, but which now form the Governor's
Summer Residence in the Campo. It is called the Fonte
da Inveja, 1882. The water comes out of a fish's mouth,
while a gilt dog's head is above. A short path leads up beyond it, shaded on both sides by bamboos, to the source of
the water; and one finds a gateway with wooden doors.
Peeping in, one sees a small stone arch with the rock below
it and a few ferns.

A little to the left of this and immediately behind the
gardens spoken of above is another called Fonte da Flora
1882. A Chinese-like building of square form, surmounted
by a vase and flowers is here. A dragon empties the water
into a stone tank in front. Above this is a square tank
with a flat top. The water is strained in this before it goes
down to the little building below. The road to these two
fountains as they are called, leads up from the direct road

to Caçilha's Bay. After passing the Barracks and a ruined
old guard-house, the road leading up between the last and
the gardens is the one to take. After going up a little way,
the Estrada, da Victoria turns off to the right, running at
at the back of the Barracks and finally running at right
angles to the road that leads up from the Campo to the
Gap. Instead of, however, turning into the Estrada da
Victoria, keep on and you come to the fountains. There are
a number of stone seats and tables here, two of the latter
being old Chinese proclamations engraved in stone, these
are turned face up and placed on two upright stones and
thus serve for tables.

"Bica de Lilau in Penha, at one time supplying water of
undoubted excellence" is ceasing to be of much public utili-
ty. "The supply from the Fonte de Felicidade in Flora
perceptably diminishes".

Many of the houses in Macao have wells inside their precincts or in the gardens attached to them.

The Flora

The Flora is the summer residence of the Governor of
Macao. It has a large garden attached to it and is at the end
of the new boulevard. It was built in 1850 by the Parish
priest, Padre Almeida and hence known then as the Padre's
Garden. It is also sometimes called the Almeida.

Green Island

Green Island is a pretty little island, at the top of the
Inner Harbour. The Jesuits held it in the early days of
the Colony, and the Bishop had a residence here afterwards.
If we forget not, some sisters of mercy had here a school.
Of recent years a causeway has been built connecting it with
the peninsula near the Barrier. Green Island (consists
principally of a little hill with a small bit of level ground
on both sides. It is now used for the Green Island) Cement
Co., for their cement works. The great fall in exchange has
benefitted this company largely, who thus, under the conditions that prevail with a low rate of exchange, can oust

their rivals in Europe and hold their own against them: though the company in the past has had much to contend against. Amongst different matters which have handicapped it in the past has been the sinking of large amounts in remidying initial mistakes and in the expenditure of large sums of money in new machinery, buildings, &c.

"The raw materials for cement are limestone and clay, of which enormous quantities are within easy reach. The first is procurable in the provinces of Kwangtung and Kwangsi; and the latter in the Inner Harbour itself, just in front of the very works * * * Most of the output goes to Manila, various ports of China, Hongkong, Japan, and other distant parts." This portland cement produced in Macao is of most superior quality, and is largely used in this part of the world.

Tamtsai and Colowan

These are two dependences of Macao and are situated on two islands to the southward, and within sight and easy reach of Macao. Two steamlaunches make the journey back and forward twice a day, starting from a small wooden landing beyond the Hongkong Canton and Macao steamer wharves in the Inner Harbour. When we took the journey some time ago the times were approximately as follows:—

Leave Macao:	Arrive at Tamtsai:	Arrive at Colowan
7 A. M.	in about	in about
11 A· M.	50 minutes.	One hour
1. P M.		and a quarter.
3 P. M.		

Leave Colowan:	Leave Tamtsai:	Arrive at Macao:
7 or 7. 30 A. M.	9. 30 A. M. or so.	in about
9 A. M.	One between the	50 minutes.
1 P. M.	above time and	
2. 30 P. M.	the next, which is at	
	1. 30 P. M.	
	2 P. M, or so.	

Starting say at 7 A. M. the boat soon leaves the Inner

Harbour and makes out for the open. Rounding the end of the Peninsula Malau Chau, Monkey Island, is seen off to the Westward on the stern quarter of the launch. On this island are situated the Imperial Maritime Customs Station. We then pass some rocks, visible at low water, the Pedra de Areia lying off the Southern end of the Peninsula. After steaming for about forty minutes or more the launch arrives at the fort on the point at Taipa. Another ten minutes and she arrives at Tamtsai when a lot of little sampans come round her to take passengers off on shore. The time the launch waits here is not sufficient to go ashore and return before she leaves for Colowan, should one wish to go on there, as the boat only stops for a quarter of an hour or so. Starting from Tamtsai we make for another island where we arrive at 8. 20 A. M., and go ashore by sampan. There is nothing much to see,—two police stations and a number of Chinese houses, shops and hovels. Saltfish is one of the staple commodities. There is a·temple to the Queen of Heaven, the sailor's patron saint, and an offering. in the shape of a model of a junk, as at the Matsopo temple in Macao. In a short time the blast of the whistle warns us it is time to hurry back, when we retrace our way to Macao. Typa and Kongpeng are two islands almost connected, the channel between them being too slightly submerged at high water to permit a steamlaunch to proceed through the passage, as the water is only about two feet deep. The view we get of Macao on the way back from Taipa is very pleasing: the City with its numerous public buildings and churches, with the Praya Grande in front, lies between two masses of hills; those crowned by the Guia Fort on the one hand, and the Penha Hills on the other.

Tamtsai situated on the Kongpeng Island has a population of say 3000 Chinese. It has a large church, which is a conspicuous object as seen from Macao.

Colowan is much smaller, having only, say 1200 or 1300 Chinese. Both of these islands are hilly. A large number of fishing junks are anchored at Tamtsai.

LAPPA

The large island on the other side of the Inner Harbour is
called Lappa. The Portuguese in the early days had some
settlements on it; but it is now entirely in the hands of the
Chinese. It "is much larger and more important than is generally supposed. The actual area is about thirty square
miles. As far as the base of the mountains its soil teams
with vegetation. Here and there is a small village, chiefly
inhabited by farmers and labourers of the lowest class. Large
tracts of land covered with paddy-fields which furnish the
industrious owners with rice of a superior quality. Cabbages,
turnips, the famous Macao potato, gourds and pumpkins,
peas and beans, are also exported from the island. Sugar-
cane, though planted in many places, does not seem able to
hold its own against the same article exported from the
riverine ports. The earth at the base of some of the Lappa
Mountains is calcareous, while that in other places is in-
termingled with soft, whitish stones". There are several
very pretty walks to be taken on Lappa rambling by Chinese
footpaths near the shores on more level ground, or wander-
ing up amongst the hills, or penetrating up the valleys, rock-
strewn with gigantic boulders, piled in the utmost confusion
one on the top of the other.

A very pretty walk may be had by taking a sampan and
crossing over to this other side of the Inner Harbour, to a
stone pier at a place called Shek-kok-tsui, Stony Point.
This landing place is nearly opposite to Camoëns' Gardens.
The time it may take to go across depends entirely upon the
state of the tide: the journey over the water may take forty
minutes, or only twenty-five. Some very fine views of Macao
and its guardian forts are obtained. Arrived on the other
side, you have the choice of several walks: you may keep
by the water's edge, or you may strike up in to a valley
strewn with great masses of boulders, left piled up in most
wonderful positions by the denudation of the soil with trop-
ical rains. These boulders covering the beds of the nullahs
are of splendid finely grained granite. Mumerous pretty
ferns are to be found, and when in season sweet honeysuckle,

rhodomyrtis, and other flowers repay one for any fatigue
from the rough walk. A curious sort of large lizard, six or
eight inches long, may be seen here. If one is about the
stumps of a bush, it looks uncommonly like a part of the
bush itself. They are not all the same colour, one seen by
the writer had its head and shoulders of one shade, while
another was entirely black and rapidly disappeared down a
hole in the earth. The Chinese say they are very poisonous.
A rickshaw coolie, whom we engaged one day, had a won-
drous story to tell about the danger of being bitten by this
lizard at a certain hour.

THE TEN TABLES

On landing on Lappa at the spot mentioned above, take
the path to the right as above, and after walking half a mile
or nearly a mile, the path, it will be seen, bifurcates. Eschew
the lower one near the water, and follow the other which
slightly trends up. After a short distance, turn up a cul-
tivated valley, reaching a mile or two into the hills and go
on to its upper end, where will be found a stream crossed
by bridges, numerous little shrines, larger buildings, winding paths, inscribed rocks, a shed with stone tables, large
enough to picnic a good company and all the other adjuncts
with which the Chinese delight to embellish a lovely nook,
already wild and beautiful in its natural state. A small
pagoda is seen up the rocky bed of the stream. The Chinese
call the place the Chuk Sin T'ung (Chook Seen T'oong),
The Grotto of the Bamboo Fairy.

THE SILVER VALLEY

This is also on Lappa; but at the Southern end, near the
entrance to the Inner Harbour. From the top of the Penha
Hills is seen on the opposite shore of the Inner Harbour a
beautiful green valley: this is the Silver Valley (Ngun Hang
in Chinese). It is a very pleasant excursion to take on the
evening of a summer's day, or the morning or afternoon of
a winter's one, the only thing to be sure of is that it is high
tide, otherwise there is a mud flat which prevents landing.
Going down to the Praya Menduca, a sampan may be hired
for twenty cents for the trip. Rowing across and down the

Harbour, in about twenty minutes, one arrives at some large rocks at the north side of a sandy beach. Landing on these, you cross them towards some native houses and follow the path which runs between these houses. In some of these houses the Chinese mȫü tsoi (mooee tsoi) or sour crout, or salt rotten vegetables, is prepared. Also some shallow tank-like places are to be seen where paddy-husks are being prepared for the purpose of being manufactured into Chinese tooth-powder, which is used to whiten the grains of rice after they have been hulled. Finally clear the inodorous habitations with their yelping curs, but still keeping at the side of the running streamlet, or rather small channel of water, with at certain seasons of the year beautiful green paddy-fields lying below you to the left, and soon seeing a stream flowing below you also on the same hand, you continue to ascend slightly, the scenery being very pretty, and beautiful ferns growing about, for a walk along this winding path for about a mile or rather more, you come to a Chinese p'ai lau, or honorific portal, which you pass through, still keeping on, but slightly more to the left and in two or there minutes you come across a bewildering confusion of boulders, piled about in all directions in the valley. If in difficulty in finding the exact spot, a native, if you can get him to understand what you want, will point it out to you. On the surface of several of these boulders, it will be noticed that certain spots have been hammered on, and these places, if struck with an iron instrument, will give out a clear metallic ring, though not with so much resonance as a bell would have. The sound is more like that produced by striking a piece of metal. The view down the valley from this spot is lovely with a peep of the sea at the end. Quarrying operations have taken place during recent years by which some of these sounding rocks have been destroyed, so that if any difficulty is experienced in finding the spot, it is well to solicit the assistance of some of the Chinese in the neighbourhood to point out those that remain.

If desired, an extension of this walk can be made by following a path running along the hill slopes at right angles

to the path from the Inner Harbour, and which strikes off
from the nighbourhood of the p'ai-lau. It is a most pleasant and interesting walk up the hill by Chinese paths.
Passing a Chinese Imperial Maritime Station, one gets a
splendid view of Macao. Then descending one soon gets on
level ground, passing a guard-house of the Customs, one
can continue the walk to the Ten Tables, by the path already described, or taking a sampan at the pier mentioned
a few pages back return to Macao.

Pak Shanleng

This is the name of the range of high hills beyond the Barrier on Chinese territory, as as well as the name of a village
of a thousand or two thousand inhabitants, situated not far
from the foot of the hills. This is about the only place by
which one can go by riskshaw out of Macao, as the road is
broad for a Chinese road. Leaving the Barrier, the path
for a few steps is through sand which is so heavy a drag on
the wheels of the vehicle that it is only fair to the men to
walk till you come to a stone (granite), paved road. Soon
after starting the road forks: that to the right leads to the
village of Shui Chung, some of the white houses of which
are seen in the distance. The road branching off to the
right is the one to be followed. Our way here is through a
perfect necropolis; for the Chinese graves are thicker than
is generally the case, and more like, in their rows upon rows,
the way in which graves are disposed in a foreign Cemetery,
though near large cities, even in China, the houses of the
dead are thus placed close together. After getting off the
isthmus, they are, however not so very abundant, though
common enough. The stone road soon ends and sandy
pieces occur every little distance, and into the ruts filled
with the loose sand, the wheels of the vehicle sink, giving
the passenger some very rough jolts.

After leaving the isthmus, the road winds through fields,
principally rice, with a small range of low hills to the right,
while the higher range looms off in the distance and further
to the north-west. Some footpaths lead to the hills off to

the right. The land is open towards the Inner Harbour, but after a while a low range rises a little way off between it and us. On one low height are the ruins of an old Chinese fort. Occasionally we cross the narrow channels of water by the small rough bridges, consisting of slabs of granite laid side by side, when the rickshaw coolie has to exercise special care to prevent the wheels of his rickshaw being caught in the spaces between the slabs. In nearly half an hour from the Barrier we reach, at a small distance from the path, a small pagoda, (a man-t'ap), which looks new, and has been rebuilt, as far as we can learn. This pagoda is visible from the Barrier. A footpath leads off to the left by which one goes to Ts 'in Shan, the Casa Branca of the Portuguese. It is about two or three miles further off. Stop at this place and give the coolies a rest under the shade of some beautiful trees and at the side of a small temple. From this spot a path also leads off by which, amongst other places, one may go to Canton. After a rest, we go to the gate of the village (which latter was built in the Ming Dynasty) in a brick wall. There is also a wall formed of rough-hewn slabs of granite, piled upon the top of each other, header and stretcher fashion, and without any cement, rising to the height of fifteen or twenty feet and the length of a slab in width. This wall surrounds a great part of the village and attests to the truth of what our jinrickshaw coolies tell us, viz., that the village is a wealthy one. Compradores and men who have been in Shanghai, Foochow, and California retire here. Many of the houses are good, and though there are poor ones, not so many as in some places.' About half an hour takes us back to the Barrier and about the same time to the Praya.

The Hot Springs

It is a pleasant and interesting trip to these at a place called Yung Mak, north-north-west of Macao and about twenty miles by steamlaunch, which has to be specially hired for the trip, unless one goes by the passenger-boat, which leaves at 8 A. M. returning at 3 P. M. If a steamlaunch is specially hired, one of those going generally to Taipa is open to a bargain.

There are three pools at the Hot Spring, but they are said to vary in number and position from time to time. And it is further stated that cold springs formerly existed there. The following short account of an excursion to them by a party, of which the author was one, may give some idea to intend-ing tourists what they are like. All preliminaries being arranged, and starting from the Inner Harbour at about 9. 15 A. M., we steam up the Harbour, close to Green Island, when we turn to the left and proceeding about half an hour from the wharf, we pass Ts'in Shan where there are three or four Chinese (native) revenue cruisers: one lot collecting kerosene dues; one for opium dues; and another for general goods. Even before we reach these vessels there are two or three Customs mat-sheds. After a while the stream nar-rows. There are high hills in the back-ground with low-lying flat ground, and bushes and groves every now and then, with villages lying at the foot of the hills, lower hills being near at hand. We pass Sha Mei, opposite a temple. In nearly an hour after leaving Macao, we enter a river, another branch coming in from the left, as the stream flows. Extensive muddy fields are on each side of the stream and the hills recede some distance back from the river. At 10.15 A. M. we turn round to the right and pass a Chinese (native) revenue-cruiser lying to the right. The scenery is pretty. Owing to the banks hiding the different channels and water-ways, boats seem to be sailing along the fields. Pretty little clumps of bamboo with mat sheds below them and low-wooded hills with temples nestling at their feet all add to the picturesqueness of the other scenery.

We arrive at our destination at 11. 40 A. M.; going up a small branch from the stream, we finally turn into a chan-nel about the breadth of the boat. Landing we walk about forty feet and get to a pool about twelve feet across and several feet deep, nearly circular, out of the centre of which bubbles are coming up. The water is as hot to the touch as a very hot bath. A narrow channel connects this with the stream.

About two minutes walk from this first one, we come to another not connected with the stream as the other was. It is about six feet across and nearly circular, a little longer than wide with bubbles rising from several places at the bottom. The water is much hotter than the other—very much hotter in fact. It runs out by a small channel, a stream rising from it. The thermometer we have with us rises as high as it can when put into this pool and not being able to rise any higher stops at 148.

One and a half minute's walk from the second brings us to the third, about eight feet by five feet in dimensions. It is clearer, connected with the outside water, and not so hot as the second one, but hotter than the first. The thermomether rises to 142. A very little stream, almost imperceptable rises from it. Occasionally a few bubbles come up from the spots on the bottom.

These three pools are situated amidst a lot of paddy fields with some huts—shanties, close to the third, an amphitheatre of hills all around. "They are situated in a valley surrounded by high mountains, and from the position of the springs at the centre of the circle of mountains it is generally considered that the site is that of an extinct volcano."

That these pools were the subject of superstition was evinced by some candles placed at one of them by the Chinese; at the same time the Chinese is nothing if not utilitarian, and in this case they turn them to account by plucking fowls at the hottest of them.

The Island of San Joao

The Portuguese first came to China in the year 1517, and at first they appear to have anchored at a port on the northwest coast of the Island of San Joao, San-cheun, San-chuenshan, San-shan, Sancian, or St. John, as it has been variously written.

Here they do not appear to have built houses, but we read of a fort having been erected, which, however, did not stand long. The port of Tamao was closed to foreign trade,

and the whole of this trade in A. D. 1554 was concentrated
at Lampacao, an island visible from Macao on a clear day.
In one of the lives of the great poet Camoens, prefixed to
an edition of his own works in his own language, it is said
that the poet lived at Lampacao, and there are good reasons for believing that the Portuguese had fixed habitations
on this island of Lampacao.

The "Great Apostle of the East," as he has been called,
and the first Jesuit missionary to China, St. Francis Xavier,
died December 1552 in sight of that land for which he so
earnestly prayed, and was buried on this island. A monument was erected to him in 1639 with the following inscription in Portuguese:—

I. H. S.

Aqui foi sepul

tado S. Francis

co Xavier doco

Panhia de Jesus

Aplodo Oriente

Este Padrao

Selevanten no

Anno

1639

There is also an inscription in Chinese.

Pilgrimages are annually made by the Roman Catholics
of Hongkong and Macao to this tomb on the saint's day.
His body, however, does not rest here now. As already
noted a large painting of his lonely death is hung in St.
Joseph's College Chapel in Macao.

The island is stated to be five leagues in length from N.
N. E. to S. S. W. Approaching it from the east, it looks as
if separated in the middle, giving rise to the supposition
that it was two islands instead of one. "There are several
bays on its north-west and eastern sides. That of Shan-
chowtong on the north-west appears to have been the one
usually frequented by the Portuguese traders, and is the
place where St. Francis Xavier was interred. It was then
called Tamao; that is according to Portuguese pronuncia-

tion Tangao, or Ta'aou, The Great Bay. The Portuguese
first traded here in 1517. In 1521 they were expelled; but
before 1542 they appear almost to have deserted it for Lampacao, to the eastward. Macao began to rise in prominence. The last mention of Lampacao states that there were
500 or 600 Portuguese living permanently there.

There is a little chapel on the island called after the saint,
doubtless, St. Francis, which was almost completely ruined
by the Chinese.

There is a village on the island and a mission-house and
chapel about a mile away from the chapel already mentioned. There is a "bust of the saint erected upon a massive
stone pedestal, about thirty feet in height, situated some
two hundred yards above the church, to mark the place
where the great saint breathed his last."

History

The history of Macao is a most interesting one. In the
first place because the Portuguese were earliest amongst
European nations to settle in China; and secondly, on account of the sturdy behavour of the Senators of this valorous
little city in asserting their rights and fighting for them. Of
course, to find the counterpart of some of the earliest Portuguese arrivals in far Cathay one must read the story of
the adventurers in our own Queen Elizabeth's time, who
sailed over sea and main fighting for the mere love of con-
quest and power to rule over others. There are two sides
to the story of how Macao came into the hands of the Portuguese as related to us by its historians. The Sweedish
Knight, Sir Andrew Ljungstedt, espoused what would be
the Chinese side of the story and proved entirely to his own
satisfaction that the severeignty of Portugal over Macao
was mythical against the opinion that had been held on the
subject. There can be but little doubt that the rights of
property were not subjected to such scrupulous criticism in
the 16th century as Lungstedt subjected them to in the
19th. Again we say that men of the stamp of the 16th
settlers at Macao, of the spirit of the English adventurers

of the period of our Queen Elizabeth, for it may be conceded at once, would not trouble their heads much as to any formal cession of territory to them. Might was right in those days and still is to a large extent. All the better, if after the material assistance rendered the Chinese against the pirates which infested the southern coast of China, the Portuguese obtained some document as written proof of tacit or or verbal permission to settle, or remain, being already settled, in Macao. The Portuguese say there was such a document; but, unfortunately the Chinese would, of course, deny it; a denial by Chinese statesmen is of no value, nor even is it unfortunately, amongst European statesmen. Knowing what we do of the Chinese, we cannot expect them to acknowledge it even if it could be produced at this day, for with the Machiavallian policy, so loved by them, it would be repudiated by Peking, if signed in Canton, or some fatal flaw would be detected, in what probably was a simple document, not ironclad against the red-hot arguments of Chinese plenipotentiaries, unless combatted by a mailed fist and a firm attitude.

Martinoe de Nello and Castro's memorandum relates that the jurisdiction of Macao extended over conquered tracts in the Höng Shan District where Portuguese owned farms and kept the Colony supplied with their products. En passant, we may remark, that on Lappa itself the Portuguese were settled on various spots, and probably even on Monkey Island; but these have all passed out of their hands, the Chinese according to the above memorandum, entered upon the conquered tracts in the Höng Shan District, the fertility of the soil being the attraction, and the mandarins resumed their jurisdiction. This seems an explicit enough statement, and Mr. Montalto de Jesus, to whom we are indebted for some of the above information, goes on to show how a bribe given to a corrupt madarin was eventually transformed into ground rent. So many different assertions have been made on the subject that the matter does not seem so clear as one would like to have it; but then many a historical subject is in a somewhat bemuddled state. For example, Ljungstedt quotes a former Bishop of Macao, who was an acting Governor of the Colony, in 1777 to this effect, that "By paying ground rent, the Portuguese acquired the temporary use and profit of Macao *ad libitum* of the Emperor." We unfortunately have not the original document before us to see whether the argument or the context alters or qualifies this statement. And we must say that Mr. M. de Jesus in his admirably written papers in "The China Review," since published with others in bookform, states in a most conclusive manner the Portuguese case.

But really the matter is of little consequence nowadays, as, if any real flaw existed in Portugal's claim to Macao, it has been rectified and all doubt set at rest by the recent treaty between Portugal and China. The question at the present day has simply an academic interest. Portugal's absorption into the Spanish kingdom in 1582 would naturally be expected to affect the relation of Macao with Europe; but while acknowledging the new condition of affairs in the mother-country, the Macaoese patriotically used their best endeavours to prevent Spanish Governors from having rule over their city and the result was the Senate, to which election was once in three years, and universal suffrage, *i. e.*, every Portuguese resident was entitled to vote by ballot for six electors, who drew up lists of persons fit to be Senators. The Chief Justice, with powers of an Administrator, from them prepared another and the final decision rested with the Vicerey of Goa, as well as the appointment of other officials. A general Council deliberated upon the most important matters, being composed of ex-senators, Bishop and clergy, Capitao de Terra, and the citizens, all the latter capable of bearing arms formed a municipal guard. The Government in Goa determined to have a company of 100 sepoys and 50 artillery, in Macao in 1784.

The revenue in these days consisted of the Customs dues which were levied in kind and sold at auction. The Charter of the Senate bears date 1586 and was issued by the Viceroy of Portuguese India. A capitao de mer Commidere also had a share in the Government of Macao, there being no Governor in these days.

We cannot follow the bold action of the Senators and people of Macao in standing up for what they considered their rights in a short account like this. "In the beginning of the eighteenth century" Governors and Captains General came from Goa, with the intention of balancing the overgrowing preponderance of the Senate. Violent party disputes arose; but the Senators generally got the better of their antagonists.

Macao was a most flourishing place in the 18th century; both the East India Company and the Dutch Company having establishment there, the former company having a library of 4000 volumes in Macao. The Chinese continued a semblance of authority, having a Custom's House in the place and taking 500 taels a year as rental from the Portuguese till 1849, when Governor Ferreira de Amaral refused to pay it any longer and drove out the Chinese officials.

In this connection the two following extracts from the Friend of China, a paper published in South China may be of interest:—

The Governor has prohibited the Chinese officers of Customs from levying duties upon goods or produce exported from Macao to ports in China, or imported from Chinese ports * * * (With the view that obtained as to the possession of Macao, the paper goes on to say) It is true that Macao was and strictly speaking is, a feudatory possession, paying an annual ground rent, or rather supposed to pay, for we believe the rent has not been collected for years, but without enquiring very minutely into the strict legality of the step, we certainly admire the independence of feeling and courage displayed by Signor Amaral. With a force of not over 200 disciplined troops and a civic guard not much to be depended upon he has, to use an American vulgarism, "regularly stumped" the Celestial Empire. The Governor vowed to put into Gaol three officials (of some rank whom Sen [the Viceroy of Canton] had appointed to investigate the circumstances connected with the deportation of the Chinese officers of Customs) if they landed in Macao (21st.

March 1849). The Governor of Macao, taking advantage. of the existing difficulties, has deported the Chinese officers of Customs who have been in the habit of collecting duties in the settlement of Portugal. He has thus declared Macao to be perpetually independent of China; the Chinese affect to look upon the Portuguese as tenants at will and until recently the Mandarins at Casa Branca exercised the right of sovereignty over the Chinese inhabitants—taxing and punishing them without consulting the Portuguese. Sen's intentions with regard to Macao are not fully known, in the meantime he has ordered all the Chinese to leave the town—which a good many of them have done and the con-tumacious Governor and the Christian inhabitants are to be starved into submission." (31st. March 1849)

This action of Governer Amaral combined with the cut-ting of new roads through some Chinese graves scattered according to Chinese custom over the hills, so incensed the neighbours that he was assassinated while he was riding with his Aide-de-camp near the Barrier. A Chinese presented a bunch of flowers to him; taking this as an act of kindness, he was taken off his guard and brutally murdered, his head being taken off and hidden in the Mong Ha Temple for a while. It is possible *more sinice* that a reward was offered for the "foreign devel's" head. His ring and the knife which was used was still in the possession of natives some years afterwards. The author's father procured the knife eventually from the Chinese and was in treaty to obtain the ring, but the negotiations fell through as doubtless the villains, or their friends, or descendants, feared that the perpetrators of the foul deed might be tracked.

Hongkong being started as a free port took away the trade from Macao with a custom House. The Portuguese authorities took steps by lowering the tariff to try and bring back the trade again, and finally it was made a free port; but unfortunately it was too late to have the desired effect.

The Coolie trade was started and had its headquarters in Macao for many years. Unscrupulous men unfortunately took it up; and it is almost well-nigh impossible with the exercise of the greatest caution to prevent the Chinese who act as gatherers together of the intending emigrants from using all sorts of tricks to beguile the innocent country folk, and entrapping many against their will, these crimps telling all sorts of lies to entice their victims. Brought into Macao, the coolies were kept in large buildings called barracoons, many of the superb mansions of the former opulent merchants being converted into these places. The whole system became so pregnant with abuses, and a mutiny and a massacre on one or two of the vessels drew a world-wide attention to these abuses and the trade was abolished in 1874. American and ships of other nationalities engaged in this coolie traffic. The Author visited an American ship lying in Macao Roads fitted up for the embarkation of these coolies in 1858 or 1859. To keep the coolies in good humour the Captain had boxes of Chinese novelettes and fiddles on board. Some of the ships were fitted out in Hongkong for this trade.

The fearful typhoon of 1874 came as another disaster to Macao, laying a considerable portion of her buildings in ruins. The elements seemed pitiless in their fury at the devoted city; for a fire broke out at the same time destroying the best houses in San Antonio Green, one of which is is still in ruins.

Much activity has been displayed of late in Macao in improvements and repairs to the streets, &c., such as the 'aying out of the Boulevard, known as the Avenida Vasco da Gama, the making of new roads, and the general embellishment of the place, amongst which may be noticed the planning of that portion of the peninsula known as the Bella Vista and Montana Russa. Here on hot evenings the inhabitants can repair for cool breezes.

A new path has been made to lead zig-zag from the Boulevard up to the centre of the range of hills running between Cacilha's Bay and the Guia Fort. Here on the top a fine view is obtained—both inland and out to sea. Dredging o the Harbour has been, or is to be, undertaken. An observatory is, we believe, also planned. But not least amongst these improvements is the clearing away of overcrowded, insanitary districts and Chinese low hovels in the endeavour to eradicate the plague, which of late years has visited, to a greater or lesser extent, Macao as well as other portions of Southern China. In 1894 while the plague was epidemic in Hongkong having newly arrived there, the greatest care was taken in the Holy City in the inspection of all incomers and no time was wasted. If any quarters were considered insanitary the most drastic measures were taken for their removal. The Macao authorities deserve the greatest praise for their promptitude and energy in their attempts to combat the plague; and no unreasoning opposition by the inhabitants were apparently allowed to baulk the wise plans of the Macao officials. The following will give some idea of the method employed:—"Some suspicion exists regarding certain parts, of China town, and in one locality, the Horta de Volong, near St. Lazarus Church, the officers of the P. W. D. have been for some days carrying on wholesale destruction, tearing up roads, opening drains, and in fact wiping the filthy quarter out of existence. Our methods here are sharp and summary; a few hours notice for the people to get out, and without further parley the work is completed.

If these plans are not interrupted in our sister Colony of Macao, before long no insanitary districts will be left in the place.

Gambling is most unfortunately licensed in Macao, large establishments being fitted up for the purpose, and with their allurements cause many fools to part with their hard-earned gains to the detriment of their wives and families and their own morals. The revenue of Macao is pretty nearly a million dollars—in 1901 it was estimated at $980,522,—and the expenditure was also estimated at $666,159.

The freedom from the squeezes of the corrupt Chinese officials in their own land and the lower rentals than those prevailing in Hongkong have all largely tended to increase the Chinese population of Macao, many men in Hongkong having houses and their families resident there.

Some of the Canton foreign firms have branches in this

pleasant Portuguese Colony, notably amongst them **Messrs.**
Deacon & Co., who are agents for the P. & O. Co., and a
number of different insurance offices, and shipping lines; and
also Messrs. Herbert Dent & Co., who are likewise agents
for a number of shipping lines and insurance offices.

There are also several Portuguese firms of general merchants and commission agents.

Numerous stores for the sale of foreign goods will be found
scattered here and there in different parts of the city. A
number of them are congregated in the Rua Central, a street
parallel with the Praya Grande and a few steps up from it
by some of the side streets.

The native quarters of Macao abound with native shops
of all kinds and descriptions.

The Portuguese support several newspapers published in
Macao in their own language; and there is one Chinese paper.

Government

Ever since therefore the days of the Governor Sr. Feireira
do Amaral when on the 12th March 1849, he ousted the last
vestiges of Chinese authority by forcibly closing out the
Chinese Custom House in Macao and snapped with a bold
hand the last links of connection with China by refusing to
continue to pay any longer the yearly rental of 500 taels to
the Canton authorities, the Chinese mandarins have had no
power nor semblance of it in Macao. We are told that to
farther accentuate the new order the same Governor also
desired the Mandarin at Macao to notify his colleagues that
they must abstain from sounding the gong—the usual Chinese notice of an official's advent—when visiting Macao, and
the Portuguese military in its place were to accord the cus-
tomary honours paid to foreign functionaries.

The Governors of Macao are appointed from Portugal and
hold besides the appointments of Ministers Plenipotentiary
to the Courts of Peking, Yedo, and Bankok. They have a
Secretary-General who is also a Secretary of Legation.

The Secretariat has a Civil and a Military Department:
the former consisting of a Head of Department and Assistant

Head and several Clerks; the latter consisting of a military commissioned officer as Head and several non-commissioned officers as clerks. The Chinese Department likewise consists of about half-a-dozen Interpreters—not Chinese, as they all bear Portuguese names. There are four Councils of which the Governor is the President. The Governors' Council consisting besides of the Secretary-General, the Bishop, the Judge, the First and Second Commandante of the Guarde Policial, the Delegado do Procueado du Coroa, the Inspector da Fazenda, the President and Chief of the Sanitary Board.

The Provincial Council consists of the Governor, the Secretary General, the Procurador da Coroa, and the Inspector da Fazenda, the President of the Senate, and Chief of the Sanitary Board (Serviço de Saude).

The Council of Public Works consists of the Governor, the Director of Public Works, the Port and the Delegado do Procurador da Coroa and Inspector da Fazenda and a Secretary. The Council of Public Instruction consists of the Governor, the Bishop as Vice-President and three members.

The Junta de Justica or Supreme Court is divided into two Sections, Civil and Military, over both of which the Governor presides, the members consisting in the former of the Judge. the two elective members of the Provincial Council, the President of the Municipal Chambers and the Procurador dos Negocios Sinicos, while in the Military Section the members consist of the Judge, the Commandant of the Police, the Capitão de Mer e Guerra, the Chefe da Estaçao Naval, and the Captain of Artillery.

The Judicial Department itself consists of a Judge, and two Deputy Judges, the Attorney General and others.

The Revenue Department, which looks after that important function of Government, serves for both Macao and Timor.

There are quite a number of other officials belonging to other Departments, such as those subordinate to the Director of Public Works with its Committee, presided over by the Governor.

There is also an Administrative Council for Macao, and another for Taipa and Colowan.

There is a Fire Brigade, a Board of Health or Sanitary Board, and a Post Office, a Chinese Department, a Harbour-Master's Department, a Police Force, and a large Municipal Chamber and Municipal Council and other Government Departments and Officials.

The Naval Force consists of two gunboats, the 'Diu', 706 tons, 6 guns and 200 horse-power and the 'Bengo' 462 tons 4 guns, and 400 horse-power and the smaller vessel 'Dilly' of 100 tons, 2 guns and 40 horse-power.

The Military have under their charge the different forts and the Military Hospital of San Januario.

The Ecclesiastical Government of the Colony is likewise pretty extensive in its organisation, headed by the Bishop, the Vicar-General, and its Vicars, Chaplains, &c, for its thirteen places of worship.

Communication

The Hong Kong, Canton, and Macao Steamboat Co's. S. S. 'Heung Shan' runs daily between Hongkong and Macao leaving the former port generally at 2 P. M. and and returning from the latter at 7.30 or 8 A. M. usually. But it would be well to inquire before starting, as otherwise one may find the steamer gone an hour before its usual time.

Starting then from Hongkong we steam rapidly out of the Harbour, the city and island showing well to advantage from the deck of the steamer, as it steers its way through the numerous ships and innumerable boats and junks which lie thick all over the waters, or sail with the wind or tack against it across from one point to another. But we rapidly leave the Harbour behind us, gliding out through the Sulpher Channel, named after H. M. S. 'Sulpher,' and dividing Hongkong from Green Island. Out in the open we make for Double Island. Pokfulum soon comes into view with its bungalows and many of those on the Peak are also seen, Passing through the wider waters, but with many islands scattered all round, some being but the upmost peaks of some sub-marine mountain, while others rear massive slopes into the air; even far away on the horizon they form a boundary to the water in one direction or another. The most of them are small, but none the less picturesque on that account.

At about 2.30 p. m. we reach Cheong Chow, or Long Island, or, as it is also called, Dumb Bell Island. This is now British, but was formerly one of the stations of the gunboats, or revenue-cruisers, of the Imperial Maritime Customs of China in the so-called blockade of Hongkong. Numerous Chinese fishing-junks are all about, plying their trade. For a couple of hours or so one skirts along the Southern shores of the large Island of Lan-tao, an island larger than Hongkong, with grand mountains culminating in a peak 3050 feet in height. The views are beautiful on a clear day. At the western end of this island is a small levelled spot on which in the early days of European intercourse with China, the Dutch are said to have built a fort. Then leaving the shelter of this island one is shortly in a bit of more open sea. Between 4 and 5 p. m. Macao's white houses are seen in the distance, after having first looked at the two I. M. Customs Stations outside the Colony. In this vicinity are the Mine Islands as well as other islands. It is a very pleasant walk out from Macao, past the shore and by inland paths to these stations. We soon pass Caçilha's Bay, the Cliff Road, the Lighthouse and rapidly nearing the Holy City, it opens out, hills and forts and churches coming into view one after the other. We admire the beautiful sweep of the Praya Grande and then, rounding the Penha Hill, the Inner Harbour comes into sight and we rapidly enter it. Monkey Island (Ma Lau Chow) with another I. M. Customs Station on it to the left, and Lappa opposite Macao. A neat little Portuguese gunboat with the beautiful Portuguese flag guards the entrance. The Bar Fort is passed, the temple of Matsopo, the Barracks, the Harbour Master's, hundreds of Chinese shops, and finally we are fastened up at the wharf, where a crowd is awaiting the arrival of the steamer, while scores of roomy rickshas are on shore, ready to wheel us off to any of the three Hotels, or wherever we want to go. The Hotels are the Boa Vista, the Macao, and the Internacional.

Another steamer belonging to the same Company leaves Macao for Canton in the early morning and Canton on the alternate days. The China Merchants' Steam Navigation Company have also a steamer or two on the line. The journey takes about seven or eight hours, or upwards, depending, of course, on state of wind and tide, &c.

Besides the steamer mentioned above there is a smaller boat that leaves Hongkong for Macao at 7 oclock every morning, returning the same day from Macao, giving the visitor an hour or two or so in Macao itself.

Jinrickshas

There are a number of these useful little vehicles plying for hire and the gradients of most of the streets are not sufficiently steep, as in Hongkong, to prevent them going up and down hill. The fares of these licensed vehicles, unless altered of late, are as follows:—

An hour, or anything short of it, within the walls of the city..5 cts.

Outside of the city walls for an hour............10 cts.

And for each extra half-hour....................5 cts.

If two get into the same rickshaw, the price to be arranged with the coolie.

Sedan-Chairs

There are about 170 of these plying for hire on the streets. They are registered like the rickshaws, and numbered, and the Bearers have also a board with the fares printed on them. If not recently altered the fares are:—

From 6 a. m. till 6 p. m.—

One hour................10 cts.

Six hours...............50 cts.

Twelve hours...........$.1.—

During the evening 5 cts. more an hour.

A Tribute to Camoens

Camoëns, noblest of thy ancient race,
Illustrious sires and noble dames thy forbears,
Adversity's stern rule thy youthful school,
A scholar thou; thy natural tastes most keen;
A warrior bold with heart of steel and thoughts
That hewed their way spite bitter adverse foes.
Till one and all now bend the rev'rent knee
Before thy shrine.   That shrine no gilded fane
That rears ambitious head aloft to cope
With brightest heaven; but buried, hid 'midst shade
Of trees and rocks.   And here thy fav'rite haunt,
What time an exile thou from Tagus' shore
And India's strand, thou past thy happiest days
Amidst these groves, thy Lusiads to pen.
Alas! that noble gifts so great as thine
Should flicker out 'midst poverty and pain.
Unknown, unwept, a pauper's grave thy fane.
It matters not where now thy dust is laid.
Immortal is thy fame: thou livest still.
Patane's sylvan shades are classic ground,
And hallowed by thy name: they form a shrine
Where all who love the poet's art shall flock,
To dream of thee and all thy glorious task,
While those who shunn'd or did thee grossest ill;
Have changed to dust forgot with all their works.

ERRATA

Page	2	line	7	for	bautiful	read	beautiful.
„	3	„	15	„	early	„	easy.
„	4	„	35	„	Cacilhas	„	Caçilhas.
„	5	„	18	„	„	„	„
„	6	„	21	before quiet insert with its.			
„	„	„	30	„	Sea	„	the.
„	7	„	38	for	Menduia	read	Menduca.
„	9	„	7	„	on	„	or
„	9	„	30	„	freeks	„	freaks.
„	„	„	„	„	Pontugal	„	Portugal.
„	„	„	34	„	Luciads	„	Lusiads.
„	„	„	36	„	like	„	to the state.
„	10	„	3	before East insert the.			
„	„	„	20	„	Luz	read	Luiz.
„	10	„	21	„	Neisceo	„	Nasceo.
„	„	„	27	„	Cantoes	„	Cantos.
„	11	„	32	„	combalidos	„	Combatidos.
„	12	„	2	„	folici	„	felici.
„	„	„	„	„	ardito	„	ardite.
„	„	„	„	„	antenno	„	antenne.
„	„	„	3	„	coutre	„	contre.
„	„	„	„	„	ripartaft	„	ripartaff.
„	„	„	„	„	giorus	„	giorno.
„	„	„	„	„	ue	„	ne.
„	„	„	5	„	caderoaceonuay	„	coltra acconuay
„	„	„	7	„	leictope	„	Ciclope.
„	„	„	„	„	chraggo	„	chraggio.
„	„	„	8	„	aygie	„	aggie.
„	„	„	13	„	statzu	„	statza.
„	„	„	14	„	foruea	„	forma
„	„	„	„	„	vessigi	„	vestigi.
„	„	„	15	„	funa	„	fama.
„	„	„	„	„	agginogo	„	aggiuago.
„	„	„	16	„	Torgunto	„	Torquato.
„	„	„	21	„	lovliest	„	loveliest.
„	„	„	25	„	cathyon	„	Cathayon.
„	„	„	33	„	Dr. Hourin	„	Dr. Bowring.
„	„	„	36	„	gruto	„	gruta.
„	„	„	38	„	sandado	„	saudado.
„	13	„	3	„	fresqui dao	„	fresquidao.
„	„	„	4	„	far	„	ia.
„	„	„	„	„	aserbus	„	acerbus.
„	„	„	6	„	mariosos	„	maviosos.
„	„	„	„	„	sous	„	sons.
„	„	„	„	„	terrivies	„	terriveis.
„	„	„	15	„	On	„	Ou.
„	„	„	„	„	modulon	„	modulou.
„	„	„	25	„	pateruels	„	paternels.
„	„	„	26	„	bellone	„	Bellone.
„	„	„	„	„	cueillet	„	cueillit.
„	„	„	34	„	J'aiuais	„	J'aimais.
„	„	„	„	„	salmer	„	saluer.
„	„	„	„	„	fegas	„	fuyais.
„	„	„	39	„	famveus	„	Camoes.
„	„	„	„	„	Domine	„	d'origine.
„	„	„	40	„	voyaeur	„	voyageur.
„	„	„	„	„	religeux	„	religieux.
„	14	„	7	„	Fronnes	„	Frondes.

69

Page	„	line	8	for	Fervebnt	read	Fervebat.
„	„	„	9	„	Camooëntis	„	Camoëntis.
„	„	„	10	„	Signnm	„	Signum.
„	„	„	„	after	*Signum* insert *et.*		
„	„	„	19	„	ingeni	read	ingenii.
„	„	„	20	„	perene	„	perenne.
„	„	„	21	„	quaerit	„	quaerit.
„	„	„	24	„	Redens	„	Spernens.
„	„	„	„	„	sepulchrorum	„	sepulchrorumque.
„	„	„	„	„	inauess	„	inanes.
„	15	„	27	„	Tazenda	„	Fazenda.
„	„	„	29	„	Procurator	„	Procurador.
„	16	„	20	„	partioned	„	partitioned.
„	„	„	22	„	opportnnity	„	opportunity.
„	17	„	5	„	En	„	Em.
„	„	„	„	after	o insert	„	Governador e.
„	„	„	6	„	d'esta	„	da.
„	„	„	7	„	Etreiro	„	letreiro.
„	„	„	„	„	le aldade	„	lealdade.
„	„	„	8	„	Conhecu	„	conheceo.
„	„	„	„	„	cidade	„	meradores.
„	17	„	11	„	entablatuer	„	entablature.
„	„	„	17	„	Secretarix	„	Secretaria.
„	„	„	35	„	Concellio	„	Conselho.
„	18	„	17	before	way insert		the.
„	„	„	25	„	Vrgini	„	Virgini.
„	21	„	3	„	Lourenco	„	Lourenço.
„	22	„	17	„	Monha	„	Mongha.
„	24	„	5	„	Vincente	„	Vicente.
„	„	„	6	„	nascao	„	nasceo.
„	„	„	16	„	his	„	has.
„	25	„	10	before	Praya insert the.		
„	„	„	24	„	Lorenzo	read	Lorenco.
„	„	„	28	„	Agostino	„	Agostinho.
„	27	„	10	„	coin	„	coign.
„	29	„	25	„	Fransco	„	Francisco.
„	„	„	32	„	Monga	„	Mongha.
„	30	„	5	„	„	„	„
„	31	„	23	„	„	„	„
„	32	„	8	„	incarceraton	„	incarceration.
„	33	„	7	„	Janario	„	Jan uario.
„	34	„	17	„	be	„	de.
„	35	„	15	„	alread	„	already.
„	37	„	15	„	Cabo	„	Caho.
„	„	„	29	before	Convent insert the.		
„	„	„	22	„	Lourenco	read	Lourenço.
„	„	„	27	„	Canosimas	„	Canocinas.
„	„	„	26	„	Italiae	„	Italian.
„	„	„	27	„	baving	„	having.
„	„	„	32	before	the insert by		
„	38	„	„	„	ba	„	da.
„	39	„	26	„	Cosa	read	Rosa.
„	41	„	18	before	Joao insert S.		
„	41	„	24	„	Cacilha	read	Caçilha.
„	„	„	29	„	Oude	„	Onde.
„	42	„	3	„	Camoens	„	Camoëns.
„	„	„	14	„	Beneniseito	„	Benenireito.

Page	42	line	18	for	Muliter	read	Militar.
,,	,,	,,	20	,,	Ordem	,,	Ordene.
,,	,,	,,	22	,,	Cacalleiro	,,	Cavalleiro.
,,	,,	,,	24	,,	Fidalho	,,	Fidaleo.
,,	,,	,,	26	,,	Farao Viscomte	,,	Barão Visconde.
,,	,,	,,	27	,,	Comamedalha	,,	Com a medalha.
,,	43	,,	2	,,	Cham	,,	Chan.
,,	,,	,,	13	before Bica insert The.			
,,	44	,,	15	,,	de	read	da.
,,	44	,,	35	,,	benefitted	,,	benefited.
,,	45	,,	5	,,	remidying	,,	remedying.
,,	46	,,	6	,,	Areia	,,	Areca.
,,	49	,,	10	after clear insert of.			
,,	,,	,,	17	,,	for	read	after.
,,	,,	,,	20	,,	there	,,	three.
Page	51	line	14	before Stop insert We.			
,,	54	,,	21	,,	Selevantem	read	Selevantou.
,,	55	,,	23	,,	Sweedish	,,	Swedish.
,,	56	,,	15	,,	Machiavallean	,,	Machiavellian.
,,	,,	,,	34	,,	Madarin	,,	mandarin.
,,	,,	,,	31	,,	Sovereignty	,,	sovereignty.
,,	,,	,,	35	,,	Lungstedt	,,	Ljungstedt.
,,	,,	,,	21	,,	Martinoe	,,	Martinho.
,,	,,	,,	,,	,,	Nello	,,	Mello.
,,	57	,,	27	,,	vicerey	,,	viceroy.
,,	58	,,	12	,,	establishment	,,	establishments.
,,	,,	,,	16	,,	de	,,	do
,,	,,	,,	36	,,	Sen	,,	Seu.
,,	,,	,,	9	,,	,,	,,	,,
,,	59	,,	15	,,	Governer	,,	Governor.
,,	,,	,,	23	,,	sinice	,,	sinico.
,,	,,	,,	25	,,	was	,,	were.
,,	60	,,	31	,,	Montana	,,	Montanha.
,,	61	,,	13	,,	were	,,	was.
,,	,,	,,	20	,,	ef	,,	of.
,,	62	,,	18	,,	Feireira	,,	Ferreira.
,,	63	,,	9	,,	Procueado	,,	Procurado.
,,	,,	,,	17	before Port insert Captain of the.			
,,	,,	,,	21	,,	Justica	,,	Justicia.
,,	,,	,,	28	,,	Mer	read	Mar.
,,	64	,,	9	,,	706	,,	729.
,,	,,	,,	,,	,,	6	,,	8.
,,	,,	,,	,,	,,	200	,,	700.
,,	,,	,,	10 & 11	,, strike out and the Bengo, 462 tons 4 guns and 400 horse power.			
,,	65	,,	22	for	Mime	read	Nine.

INDEX.

A.

B.

G.

N.

O.

P.

T.